THE MILKSHAKE DETECTIVES

Also by Heather Butler

Us Minus Mum

THE MILKSHAKE DETECTIVES

Heather Butler

LITTLE, BROWN BOOKS FOR YOUNG READERS
www.lbkids.co.uk

LITTLE, BROWN BOOKS FOR YOUNG READERS

First published in Great Britain in 2015 by
Hodder & Stoughton

Text copyright © 2015 by Heather Butler

A CIP catalogue record for this book
is available from the British Library.

ISBN 978-0-349-124-100

Typeset in Stone Serif by M Rules
Printed and bound in Great Britain by
Clays Ltd, St Ives plc

The paper and board used in this book are made
from wood from responsible sources.

MIX
Paper from
responsible sources
FSC® C104740

Little, Brown Books for Young Readers
An imprint of Hachette Children's Group
Part of Hodder and Stoughton Limited
Carmelite House
50 Victoria Embankment
London EC4Y 0DZ

An Hachette UK Company
www.hachette.co.uk

www.hachettechildrens.co.uk

CHAPTER 1

Moving to 3, Dead End Lane is meant to be a lovely new start. It's not, though, because I have the tiniest bedroom imaginable and Mum's hung my old Peppa Pig curtains in the window.

"We'll buy new ones for you as soon as we can afford them," Mum says, as Max builds brand-new bunk beds in Rhino and Germery's big bedroom at the front of the house. They might be five and seven but they've got a new carpet in there as well, and a card from Kelly. The card reads:

Dear Ryan and Jeremy,
I hope you're happy in Peddle-Worth. If you're good I'll buy you both a new football shirt.
Love Mummy xx

All anyone's bought me are some *Mystery: Solved* stickers for my old chest of drawers. I need them because Penelope Pink (my favourite character from *Mystery: Solved*) has to guard my room from Rhino and Germery. The two of them got hold of Bertie, my teddy bear, and tried to stretch him. I pretended not to care; but if those little doughnut-heads think they can mess with my stuff they are sooo wrong.

Max, Mum and I unpack boxes. Germery and Rhino go outside and ride their bikes up and down Dead End Lane. They meet William Holdsworth, who lives at number eleven, and Germery invites him back to ours. The three of them sit in the living room playing on the PlayStation, eating biscuits and doing blow-offs into the carpet.

"If you have biscuits, use a plate, please," Mum says. "It saves crumbs from going on the carpet." Germery looks at her like she is a slug with an extra head. She puts three plates on the floor next to them.

The plates are still there an hour later. Unused.

I go to school the next day and my new teacher, Mrs Winter, shows me where to sit and asks Julia Sopton to look after me. There is William Holdsworth, on my table, picking his nose and staring at me.

"Ignore him," Julia says. "He'll want you to call him Will.i.am, he doesn't believe in fairies and licks his armpits. He's gross."

"He lives in our road," I say.

"Ugh. Bad luck," Julia says.

After playtime, as we walk back to our classroom, Mrs Winter asks me if everything's all right and I say it is. "Except I'm usually called Charlie Smith and not Charlotte Smith."

"OK, glad you told me," Mrs Winter says and glances over her shoulder at William Holdsworth. He was in trouble at playtime for climbing up a drainpipe and knocking on the staffroom window. How stupid is he?

As soon as I get home, I do my homework. Mum's making macaroni cheese for supper.

We're having that because it's something Rhino will eat without fussing. I don't like macaroni cheese, even when Mum puts bacon in it. Today she makes my favourite chocolate brownie pudding as well.

Max comes home early to see how we got on at Peddle-Worth Village Primary School. The village was once called Peddleworth (without a hyphen), but when the dual carriageway was built through it, one half was called Peddle and the other half Worth.

"So your days were good?" he asks, reaching for the tomato ketchup.

"School was good, but here someone's dribbled on the toilet seat," I say.

Mum tells the boys to lift the seat up, but they ignore her. Max tells them as well, but that doesn't make any difference.

"I think," Mum says, looking at Rhino and Germery, "the downstairs toilet should become a LADIES ONLY toilet. You and your dad can use the upstairs one."

"Aaawww!" Germery says. "That's not fair."

"It's not fair on Charlie or me, either," Mum says. What a RESULT!

After supper, Mum and I take over the downstairs loo. We put photographs of me and her, and pictures of Penelope Pink and Sabrina Scarlett (my other favourite agent from *Mystery: Solved*) on the wall. Then Mum puts our fairy box under the sink. We brought it from the flat. It's a place where injured fairies recover. It's also a place where Mum and I leave messages for each other.

While we decorate the loo, Rhino and Germery sit on the sofa with Max. They each have a packet of salt and vinegar crisps. There's a football match on and they are going to shout at the telly.

"Want to join us?" Max asks me.

"No," I say. "I hate football."

"That's a shame," he says. "We love it, don't we, boys?"

"You bet we do," Rhino shouts. "Come on Man U!"

"West Ham are rubbish!" Germery says. A bit of crisp spits out of his mouth and lands on the arm of the sofa. He leans over, sticks his tongue out and licks it up. He is sooo disgusting!

Man U score a goal after fifteen minutes and

the three of them shout and scream and hug each other.

Five minutes later, West Ham score. Joe and Sheila, who live next door and must support West Ham, shout so loudly we hear them through the wall.

Mum and I are in the kitchen decorating cupcakes and think it's really funny.

"Boys," Max says, "if Man U score again, we shout like we have never shouted before. Got it?"

"Yes, Dad," they say, and come into the kitchen to find saucepans with lids to bang and clash.

"I hope Man U don't score," Mum whispers to me. AND THEY DON'T!

Moving house also meant Mum changed her job. She now works at the village shop. It's not a big shop but somehow they manage to sell all the important things people want, like chocolate and loo rolls and cards and newspapers. They even have tables outside under a striped awning. You can sit there and have a cup of tea looking out at the duck pond on the village green. The owners, Billy and Maria, let me stack shelves and fetch things if Mum is working there. I love that. It's a me-and-Mum thing because stinky-poo, badly behaved boys are NOT allowed to help. Also, Billy and Maria think Manchester United are rubbish, so that proves they have good taste.

They want to run a proper café, so there's building work going on to make one upstairs. Maria lets me help her try out recipes for the cakes and biscuits and I love doing that. Going to the shop *almost* makes me think Peddle-Worth could be an OK place to live. But then I remember Rhino and Germery live here as well, and that is a million miles from being OK. So I write notes to Mum in the fairy box, like:

Dear Mummy,
 I wish we were still living in the flat, just you and me.
 Love,
 Charlie xxxxxx

She writes back:

Dear Charlie,
It will get better.
Love,
Mum xxxxxxx

CHAPTER 2

Julia Sopton used to be best friends with Mia Hadley; only Mia Hadley's mum and dad moved when the council built the dual carriageway. So Julia and I are now best friends. That's why, when Billy and Maria decide to sell milkshakes at the shop, I phone her up.

"They want us to be the first people to try the milkshakes," I say. "We have to be at the village shop at half past nine on Saturday morning."

Maria and Mum put the milkshake blenders on the counter where they serve coffees and teas and cakes.

"Choose your flavour," Maria says. "Today we have chocolate, strawberry or banana."

"Chocolate, please," Julia says.

"Strawberry, please," I say, because I always go for pink things if I can.

Maria pushes a wisp of grey hair behind her ear. Her eyes narrow as she looks at Mum. "You do strawberry; I'll do chocolate. GO!"

"Is this a race?" Mum asks.

"Yes. And I've already started!" Maria laughs as she dives into the fridge to find a bottle of milk.

Mum picks up a box with 'Strawberry Milkshake Mix' written on the side. She flips the lid open, spoons a heaped tablespoon of powder into her blender then zips over to the freezer and pulls out a tub of strawberry ice cream. But she struggles to get the lid off.

"Slow coach!" Maria laughs.

"Charlie," Mum says, "grab the ice cream scoops so Maria can't use them."

There are three ice cream scoops in a plastic jug. I dart out my hand to get them but Julia beats me to it.

"Lightning reactions!" Maria says as Julia

gives one of the scoops to her, then hugs the jug so I can't get at it.

She thinks she is SO clever, but she's not: I jerk my finger towards the ceiling, and Julia's head goes back to see what I am pointing at. As she does, my other hand lunges for one of the scoops.

"Nice move, Charlie!" Mum laughs. She's managed to wrestle the ice cream tub lid off and now scoops some ice cream out. But Maria's chocolate mix is buzzing and whirling in the blender and—

"I win!" Maria grins as she empties her blender into a tall glass.

"You won because you cheated," Mum says with a laugh as she tips her blender upside down and pink milkshake runs out into another tall glass. "Do you want cream and chocolate sprinkles?" she asks, and Julia and I both nod.

"With fresh strawberries?" Maria asks.

"Or fresh orange?" Mum says.

I have two slices of orange and Julia has a strawberry.

Maria gives us each a straw. "Now drink them and tell us what you think," she says.

"Shall we take them outside?" Julia asks me. There is a table inside, but outside is better because we can talk without anyone hearing us.

"That's a good idea," Maria says, giving us a tray.

As we settle down at a table outside, Julia says, "You know you pointed at the ceiling to make me look up so you could grab the ice cream scoop?"

I nod.

"How did you know to do that?"

"Penelope Pink does it in episode four of series one of *Mystery: Solved*," I say.

"I knew it!" Julia says. "You love that programme, don't you?"

"I do," I say. "It's my absolute favourite."

"Mia and I used to dress up as Agents Sabrina Scarlett and Angelica Blue," Julia giggles.

"I'm always Penelope Pink," I say, and tell her about the *Mystery: Solved* detective agent pack I got for Christmas.

"I got that as well!" Julia says, and we are both laughing and know we are going to be best friends FOR EVER.

"What's your milkshake like?" I ask her.

"Yummy yummy," she says. "What's your like?"

"It's nice," I say, "but I wish I'd gone for chocolate."

"Do you want to try some of mine?" she says.

I do, and it's definitely nicer than the strawberry one.

"Emily would like yours," Julia says. "She's strawberry mad." Emily is Julia's little sister and sooo cute.

"Rhino and Germery would suck milkshake up in their mouths and then blow it out again," I say.

"They're disgusting," Julia says.

"You know they're not my real brothers, don't you?" I say. "They're Max's, and visiting their mum this weekend. It's SO nice not having them ponging the place out."

"Do you go and stay with your real dad?" Julia asks.

I shake my head

"What? Never?"

"He left when I was a baby. It's always just been me and Mum."

Actually, I wish it still was.

CHAPTER 3

Tracy (that's Julia's mum) invites me and Mum for supper. I'm excited about going, but also annoyed because Rhino and Germery are coming as well.

"Ryan, use a fork, please," Mum says as he shovels a fish finger in his mouth with his fingers. He looks at Mum like she is a smushed-up banana, then at Emily who is sitting next to him. His left hand hovers over his plate as he squelches a load of baked beans in his fingers.

Then he stuffs them in Emily's face.

"Ryan!" Mum says, and you can tell Max isn't here because she uses her really, really cross voice. "Stop that. Now."

Emily doesn't like having baked beans stuffed in her face. She picks up her spoon and thwacks Rhino on the nose. I want to hug her because she has done what I would love to do; and because she is only three, she won't get in trouble for doing it.

Mum lifts Rhino off his chair.

"You're coming with me to talk about this," she says. Rhino tries to kick her but kicks the chair instead.

"If you hadn't tried to kick me, you wouldn't have hurt yourself," Mum says. "So stop crying." She carries him out of the room as Tracy tells Emily that spoons are for eating with and not hitting other people.

"Naughty spoon," Emily says.

"It's not the spoon that's naughty. It's you."

"Me not naughty," Emily says.

Germery goes, "Want more juice."

"I'll get you some in a minute," Tracy tells him, but Emily wants him to have juice now, so throws her plastic cup at him.

SPLOOOSH!

Juice drips down Germery's face and neck and I could hug Emily all over again. But I don't.

Instead, Julia and I eat our food in an extra-sensible sort of way while Tracy cleans Germery's face.

Emily sings, "Naughty spoon, naughty cup, naughty boy."

Emily is my favourite three-year-old EVER!

As soon as Julia and I finish eating we go into the living room to watch episode twelve of *Mystery: Solved*, series two. I've only got the DVD of series one. As we watch it I have THE most brilliant brainwave.

"Julia," I say slowly, as the idea buzzes into shape. "I bet we could do that."

"Do what?"

"Solve mysteries. With our own detective agency. Here, in the village."

Julia raises her eyebrows, just like Sabrina Scarlett does, and I know I've said exactly the right thing.

"WOAH! What a fantastic idea! We'll need code names, and a bag each with our detective kits in them."

"And the right clothes," I say, thinking that I'll need a new pink top to wear.

"You could be Agent C and I'll be Agent J," Julia says.

I nod and say, "That's a great idea. And we'll need a really good name for the agency, too."

Agent J's eyes swivel from side to side as she thinks. I think too. My eyes stay completely still. But neither of us can think of a name.

"I've just thought of something," Agent J says. "One of the ducks on the pond keeps pulling its front feathers out with its beak."

What has that got to do with being a detective?

"Think *Mystery: Solved*, series one, episode one," she says. "The agents rescued a cat from a tree to see if they were any good."

"Small before tall," I whisper, which is what Penelope Pink says when she is looking for every tiny clue. "Which duck is pulling its feathers out?"

"The brown one."

"Billy calls that one Ugly," I say. "The other one's called Donny. They come in the shop and try to peck him. But why is Ugly pulling her own feathers out?"

"Don't know," Agent J says. "That's our first challenge! Let's go and find those ducks."

We both giggle and know this is the best thing EVER to do on a Thursday evening.

CHAPTER 4

Peddle-Worth is a great village to be a detective in. It's small, and everyone seems to know each other. Best of all though, Agent J and I are allowed out by ourselves, which is obviously very important for detective activities.

The village pond is next to Julia's house. Right now, Donny and Ugly are not gliding across the pond, and they're not under the massive oak tree next to it either. All we find is a feather lying on the ground.

Agent J drops the feather in an evidence bag from her *Mystery: Solved* detective kit.

"Where shall we look next?" I ask.

Agent J replies, "Let's go to the churchyard."

"Isn't that by Stevie Proctor's house?" I say and watch her blush. One of the first things I knew about Julia is that she fancies Stevie LIKE MAD.

"I don't fancy him," she says. And I think, *Chickens don't lay eggs, either.*

We look in the churchyard, but there's no sign of the ducks. There's no sign of Stevie either, so we carry on walking to the playing field, where two men I don't know are putting new nets on the goal posts.

"Who are they?" I ask Agent J.

"Mr Kahn is the one with the jogging bottoms on," she says. "He runs the football team. The other man is Arthur Rivers' dad."

"Who's Arthur Rivers?"

"Year six. Did the music for assembly last week."

I nod. I remember him now. "The ducks might be on the footbridge," I say. They often go there to quack at cars on the dual carriageway.

Quacking at cars is exactly where the ducks are. When they see us, they honk at us instead. I study Ugly's feathers. The ones on her front are fluffy and soft. I try to think like Penelope Pink would.

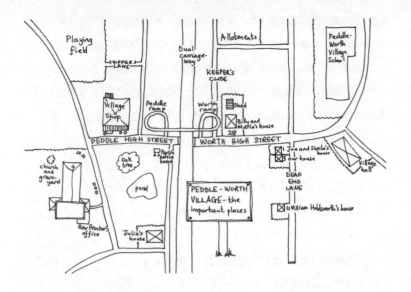

PENELOPE PINK: All you need are the right questions, Agent C.

AGENT C: We'll need evidence as well, to prove our answers.

PENELOPE PINK: Evidence is the most important part of solving a mystery.

"Do ducks use their feathers to build a nest?" I say.

"Don't know," Agent J says. "But they do build nests in spring and it's spring at the moment." Then she squeals. "Maybe they're going to have some tiny little ducklings!"

We go back to her house and check on the internet. We were right! Ducks use their own feathers to build their nests. Agent J takes out her *Mystery: Solved* notebook and writes:

MYSTERY ONE: The Ugly Duck's Feathers

She sticks in the feather we found by the oak tree and writes:

Wednesday 15th March
MYSTERY SOLVED

Underneath, we both sign our names.

Agent J

Agent C

"We started small," I say. "Next time we go tall."

"Agents Pink and Scarlett meet in a coffee shop," Agent J says. "Where is our detective agency going to meet?"

"What about the village shop?" I say. "We could buy milkshakes and sit outside and no one will ever guess we are highly trained members of a detective agency."

"Good idea, Agent C," Agent J says.

"And I've just thought of a name!" I screech, and it's THE BEST NAME EVER. "We are," I announce dramatically, "the Milkshake Detectives!"

WHIZZLING-WHOOZLES! THE MILKSHAKE DETECTIVES!

"I love it!" Agent J squeals and just for that moment I am SO glad we came to live in Peddle-Worth village.

Then I think about Germery and Rhino and I'm not quite so glad.

CHAPTER 5

FADE IN:

EXTERNAL LOCATION - THE VILLAGE
SHOPFRONT - SATURDAY MORNING

Church clock chimes ten o'clock.
AGENT C and AGENT J sit at a
table outside the village shop.
Chocolate milkshakes are on the
table. The agents appear to be
chatting but are really watching
the bridge, Peddle High Street
and the pond, looking for a
mystery that needs solving.

REVEREND PROCTOR approaches,
wearing a long coat and wellies.

AGENT J

[Urgently]

Agent C, Rev Proctor is looking
highly suspicious.

AGENT C

[Turning her head]

Is she hiding anything inside her
long coat?

AGENT J

[Trying not to giggle]

Yes. She's dressed as a sumo
wrestler.

FADE OUT

Rev Proctor is in charge of the church. If we
were playing Cluedo, she would be called Rev
Green; but she's not, she's in Peddle-Worth and
her son is in our class at school.

"Stevie," I whisper to Agent J. "Where are you?"

"I told you, I don't fancy him any more," Agent J says. *Water doesn't come out of taps, either.*

"Don't you?" I say. "Why not?"

"His legs are too skinny."

"Who do you fancy, then?" (She always fancies someone.)

"Oliver Garston. He's got nicer hair." I try to remember what Oliver's hair is like because a good detective should notice these things. I think it's brown, the same colour as Stevie's. I must check on Monday.

As we slurp the last dregs of our chocolate milkshakes, two people we have never seen before walk up Peddle High Street and go into the shop. The woman is carrying a map and the man has a large spot halfway up his nose.

"Who are they?" Agent J whispers.

"No idea," I say. Well-trained agents do not need to talk about what to do when strangers enter shops. As one, Agent J and I slide off our chairs and follow them inside. Agent J peels off to the left and stands by the freezer. I stand by the tins of custard as the man lifts a postcard out of the wire rack.

"This will do," he says in a husky voice, and walks to the counter where Maria is. "Lovely village," he continues. "And we're fascinated by the Great Peddle-Worth Bear Hunt."

Agent J's eyes meet mine as Maria laughs and says, "Those notices appeared on lamp posts last night."

MAQUITO-FALEEKO! SOMETHING MYSTERIOUS IS GOING ON IN PEDDLE-WORTH!

Without a sound, Agent J and I glide towards the shop door. Agent J opens it, we exit the shop and then race down Peddle High Street in the direction the man and woman came from. The notices must be down there somewhere.

They are, stuck to three lamp posts on bright blue paper:

BEWARE!

COMING TO A VILLAGE NEAR YOU!

THE GREAT PEDDLE-WORTH BEAR HUNT!

That is all. No dates. No details. No nothing. "What sort of bear?" Agent J says.

"Teddy bear. Grizzly bear. Cuddly bear. Koala bear."

"A koala's not a bear," Agent J says. "A koala's a koala."

"Oh," I say, and feel a bit stupid. "But whatever it is, it's coming to a village near us."

"That really means this village," Agent J says. "A bear's coming to Peddle-Worth. It's coming to get us!"

"But we don't know when," I say. "And we don't know how or why. Or what it will wear."

"It won't wear anything," Agent J says. "Bears don't wear clothes. Bears are bare!"

We walk back to the shop and sit down next to a pink plastic flamingo with a nasty-looking beak.

Billy bought it to try and scare Donny and Ugly away. "If those ducks don't stay away from my shop," he said, when he put it out, "I'm going to catch them, dump them in a box and take them to the Chinese takeaway."

I think he was joking because if there is any stale bread he gives it to children so they can feed the ducks.

Billy's put a notice by the pink plastic flamingo. It says:

Dear Ducks,

Please stay in your pond.

Signed,

The Management

Today we are not thinking about the ducks or the plastic flamingo though, because we are both writing in our *Mystery: Solved* notebooks.

The Great Peddle-Worth Bear Hunt

And then my pen conks out. So Agent J lends me her pink gel pen. I write the words 'Bear' and 'Hunt' in pink. Everything else is written in blue.

That night I lie in bed and whisper to Bertie (who does not like being stretched). "The Milkshake Detectives have a real mystery to solve!" I tell him. "It's like a mystery made just for us." Bertie doesn't say anything back. He never does, but I know he is wishing Germery would stop knocking on the wall between our bedrooms.

Germery says if he doesn't knock he can't get to sleep.

CHAPTER 6

In assembly, Mrs Sharp, the head teacher, reads from a piece of blue paper. As she does, Julia and I look at each other and our eyes get bigger and bigger.

In the village is a bear,

Follow the clues to find its lair.

If you are so very wise,

You could win yourselves a prize.

"I understand," Mrs Sharp says, "that notices have appeared on lamp posts in the village about a Bear Hunt." Lots of us nod and know what she is talking about. "Bears," she says, "are usually very shy animals. But one of them has asked me to read you the first clue." Agent J and I sit up really tall to help us listen extra hard. Mrs Sharp pushes her glasses up her nose and reads:

Oldest bark is where you'll find
Something small that will wind.

Someone in Year 6 puts up their hand.
"Yes, Kieran?" Mrs Sharp says.
"What's the prize?" he asks.
"It's a lovely prize. Something totally unique," she replies, and smiles mysteriously. "I'm not saying any more, but I'll pin the clue on the school notice board. Good luck! And keep your eyes peeled for a glimpse of the Bear!"
"I'd love to know what the prize is," Agent J whispers, as we walk back to our classroom.
"And me," I whisper back. Now it's not just the Milkshake Detectives trying to solve the Bear Hunt mystery – it's everyone else as well, and I really, really want to win the prize, whatever it is.

"We have to be the first ones to work out the answers," Agent J says as we sit down at our table.

William Holdsworth burps and takes out his pencil case.

We ignore him because he's stupid.

At playtime, Hollie says, "I think the bear clue is about the oldest dog in the village." Her nan has a very old poodle with one of those leads that winds in and out.

"That's too obvious," Agent J whispers to me. "You have to look at what's in front of you." (Sabrina Scarlett says that all the time.)

"So what is in front of us?"

"Dunno yet," she whispers, "but I do think the Milkshake Detectives should have their own logo with a fingerprint on it."

"And a milkshake," I say, and my heart does a funny little flutter because this is sooo exciting!

That afternoon, as I label a diagram in my science book of how blood flows around our bodies, my brain goes PING! and I think, *Bark grows on trees, and by the pond opposite the village shop is a very old oak tree. Maybe there is something in the tree that winds up.*

"That is genius," Agent J whispers when I tell her. So, at home time, we charge down Worth High Street, over the footbridge and on to the grass where the oak tree is.

Billy is standing in his shop doorway as we run past, and he waves at us.

We can't see anything at first, but good detectives never give up until all lines of enquiry have been explored. So we walk right around the oak tree twice and there, hidden inside a crack in the gnarled bark, is a garden gnome holding a fishing rod! Hanging from the fishing rod is a piece of blue paper with writing on.

Agent J reads:

Hedge your bets!

It could be Old Trafford

And we're cheering on the game.

"What does that mean?" she asks.
"No idea. What's Old Trafford?"
"We'll have to check on my laptop."

"Good idea," I say. As I do, Arthur Rivers and Jack Halford from Year 6 arrive on their bikes. They've worked out the clue as well.

"We were here first," Agent J says, and smiles at Arthur Rivers as he reads the words on the blue piece of paper out loud.

"Well, I know where that is," he says with a laugh.

"So do we," Agent J says, but I'm thinking, *No, we don't.* "It's so obvious," Agent J carries on.

"We'll see you there then," Jack says.

"We're not going there now," Agent J says. "We've got to do something first, haven't we, Charlie?"

I nod and say, "Yes."

We've got to find out what 'Old Trafford' is, because at the moment we haven't got a clue what it means.

CHAPTER 7

I don't go back to Julia's because her grandparents are visiting. So I walk back home. I want to tell Mum all about the Bear Hunt but can't because she is with the stinky baboons in the living room.

"Five minutes' reading, that's all you've got to do," she says to Rhino.

"Not doing it," he says back.

"Our real mum says homework is stupid," Germery says.

"Why don't I read your book to you first, then you can read it after," Mum tries again.

"I'm still not doing it," Rhino says.

"OK," Mum says. "I'm going to write in both your home-school books that you refused to read with me. I am not getting stressed about it."

We don't talk about the Bear Hunt until supper time.

"Julia's dad was in the shop today," Mum says, as she cuts up Rhino's food. "He works for *The Herald* and is going to print the clues the Bear leaves around the village in the newspaper."

"Mrs Sharp told us about the Bear Hunt," Germery says. "She read a clue but I didn't get it."

"What was the clue?" Max asks.

"Can't remember," he says.

"The clue," I say, "was 'Oldest bark is where you'll find, something small that will wind.' Julia and I worked it out and went to the oak tree by the pond where there's a gnome with a fishing rod and the next clue."

"Which is . . . ?" Max asks.

"'Hedge your bets. It could be Old Trafford and we're cheering on the game.'"

"Old Trafford, we love you!" Germery shouts. His mouth is full of potato and some of it spits out all over the table.

"What's Old Trafford?" I ask.

Max leans forward and whispers, "Charlie, it's where the greatest team in the world play."

"That must be West Ham!" Mum says, and she is smiling at Max, who pulls a face back at her like he used to do when they first started going out.

"You're so stupid," Germery says to Mum.

"Excuse me! I don't think I am," she says, and the smile on her face has melted to a frown. She blinks twice, takes a deep breath and says, "The bear posters said there was a prize at the end of the Bear Hunt. What do you think that might be?"

"Money," Germery says.

"And if it was money, what would you buy?" Mum asks. "I'd buy a seat for our garden so we could sit outside."

Max says he would buy a new headrest from eBay for his BMW, and I say that I would buy new curtains for my bedroom.

"I'd get a telly," Germery says, "for our bedroom."

"You wouldn't," Mum says. "No one is having a telly in their bedrooms."

"We have a telly in our other bedroom," Germery says.

"Well, you're not having one here." Mum looks at Max and adds, "Are they?"

"I don't know," Max says.

"They're not," Mum says. "There are things on television that aren't suitable for children to watch."

"We saw a film called *Reach for the Zombie* last weekend," Rhino says. "The zombies had big tummies that burst open."

"You are five years old and your brother is seven years old and you should not be watching films like that," Mum says.

"Our real mum says it's all right," Germery says. He sticks a fork full of mashed potato into his mouth, lifts his glass to his lips and spits the potato into it. His water now has bits of white floating in it. "When I phone her next, I'm going to tell her I want one."

He will as well. Rhino and Germery have a

mobile in a blue case so they can phone her whenever they want to.

"That's enough, Jezzie. Eat your supper," Max says as Mum whispers, "Thank you for your support, Max. Much appreciated."

As soon as I can, I text Agent J.

> Old Trafford is where Man U play football. Is the Bear clue about the playing field?

She writes back:

> I think you are right, Agent C.

The next day, straight after school, we race to the playing field. When we pass the oak tree, three children are staring at the fishing rod gnome.

"Everyone knows that clue now," Agent J says. She's right, because five other children are also at the playing field searching the hedge, and behind the hut and in the car park. There's nothing there, but while we search, Agent J and I talk about the prize (again).

"Could it be a trip to see grizzly bears in Canada?" I say.

"No way!" Agent J says. "Too expensive. I think the prize is something like a ruler with a picture of a bear on it."

"Hope it's more exciting than that!" I say back. "Mrs Sharp said it was something lovely and totally unique. A ruler's not unique, is it?"

I would sooo love us to win whatever the prize is.

CHAPTER 8

Kelly hasn't found time to take Rhino and Germery to buy new football shirts, so she's given them money and my mum has to buy the shirts instead.

We go to town straight after school. Mum gives us a drink and a biscuit in the car. As she does, Germery does a mega-sized blow-off.

"Jeremy, you could have held that in," Mum says.

"I couldn't," he answers back. "It wanted to escape."

"Far-ty par-ty!" Rhino shouts. "I'm going to do one as well."

I am SO glad I'm sitting in the front of the car

with Mum and not with those gorilla-faced farting numbskulls stinking out the back.

Mum parks the car and helps Rhino put money in the ticket machine. Then she takes his hand so he doesn't run off. If it was just Mum and me, we would be chatting to each other, but she can't chat today because she has to tell Rhino and Germery to stop throwing themselves around and not scratch their bottoms in public. She doesn't have enough words to talk to me.

"I want a drink," Rhino shouts as we pass a coffee shop.

"And me," Germery joins in.

"You had drinks and biscuits in the car," Mum says.

"Our real mum would get us one if she was here," Rhino shouts.

I sometimes wonder what Kelly is actually like. The boys have a photograph of her in their bedroom. She has curly brown hair and a big smile on her face. But she doesn't DO the things my mum does.

"You have a choice," my mum says. "We buy football shirts or we go home."

Rhino squirts bubbly spit between his teeth

and makes a grunting noise like he is doing a poo. Mum turns and walks away, towards where the sports shop is. I go with her.

"Don't turn around," she says to me, stopping in front of a shop that sells sheets and curtains.

There's something detective-like about the shop window, because we can see Max's stinkers reflected in the glass.

"It's like we've got eyes in the back of our heads," Mum whispers as the boys wonder what to do next.

"While we're waiting for them, you could buy me some new curtains," I say.

"Charlie, we'll buy you some as soon as we can," she says and I sigh, loudly, so she can hear me and know how much I hate my Peppa Pig curtains.

And now Rhino and Germery are walking towards us. The shop next to us has tellies in the window. The boys stop when they reach it.

"I want one of those," Germery says, pointing into the shop.

Beside me, Mum whirls around, then strides towards Germery. "I am *not* going to let you have a telly in your bedroom," she says firmly, bending over so she is face to face with him. "Let it go."

"My real mum," Germery shouts back, "says she'll let me have one and you can't do anything about it."

The muscles on Mum's face freeze, then she grabs Rhino's hand and marches us to the sports shop where the boys buy their Manchester United football shirts, even though they are disgustingly behaved.

We go to a clothes shop next. Germery sticks his head inside a T-shirt hanging from a hanger, pretending to be a zombie alien.

I go to the girls' section and THERE IT IS, waiting for me, as if Penelope Pink had picked it for me herself.

POODLE-WHOOSHKIN!

It's my size and it's a deep shade of pink and I love it. I love it! I LOVE IT!

Mum's looking at pyjamas with Rhino. He's having a new pair to help him stop wetting himself.

"Mum, I'm going to try this on," I call out to her, holding up the top.

"That'll look really nice on you," she says. "Love the colour." She smiles at me and I smile back and, just for a second, all she thinks about is me.

On the way back to Dead End Lane we take Germery to the playing field. He's joining Peddle-Worth's junior football team and they practise on Wednesday evenings at 5.30. They play matches on Saturdays, so Germery can only make every other week, as Kelly says there is NO WAY she can get him back to Peddle-Worth for a ten o'clock kick off.

I recognise some of the team: William Holdsworth, Stevie, Oliver and Arthur Rivers from Year 6. *Better not tell Julia*, I think, *or she'll want to come and watch them.* She might find out about them being here though, because her dad is talking to Mr Kahn and taking photographs of the players.

Mum collects Germery an hour later. He is very excited because Arthur Rivers looked along the hedge around the field and found a football with a bear drawn on it and the next clue.

SHAMOOKA-WOOKS! The Milkshake

Detectives were right about the place, but we were just too early! Then I think, *But we did send a spy – in the form of Germery – so we knew about it almost as soon as the footballers did.*

Even better, our spy remembers what the next clue is:

> For parties and meetings and Tumbling Tots,
>
> When they're not there, the door is locked.

I text Julia:

> We were right. Germery's football team found a football with a bear on it in the hedge.

Then I tell her the clue.
She texts back:

> Well done, Agent C. Tumble Tots is in the village hall. Emily goes. We can look on the way to school tomorrow.

As I read her text I think, *At the moment, we're waiting for clues to appear. Why don't the Milkshake Detectives work out WHO THE BEAR IS? Then we can track him or her down and be the first to get the clues and be more likely to win the prize, whatever it is.*

I phone Julia to tell her because this is a really important thought. She agrees with me and says it's what the Milkshake Detectives should do.

CHAPTER 9

Max works at a marketing company, so when
Rhino and Germery are getting ready for bed, I
ask him if he could design a logo for the
Milkshake Detectives.

"A detective agency?" he says. "Now that
sounds interesting. Is that to work out all these
clues the Bear keeps leaving?"

"Sort of," I say, and I am about to tell him
what the logo needs to have on it when Rhino
shouts from upstairs because he's done a poo
and there's no toilet paper left.

"Be back in a minute." Max sighs and stands
up. If boys weren't here, it would still be like
when he and Mum started going out.

The first time he visited our flat, Max spilled soup down his shirt and Mum lent him her biggest jumper. It had stripes on it. Max decided it made him look French so insisted on speaking in a French accent. THE WHOLE DAY. He was always doing daft things like that, and when I found out his favourite food was Chinese takeaway (the same as mine), I decided he and Mum were a match made in heaven. I left her a fairy box message:

Dear Mum,
    I am cool about you going out with Max. He is OK.
    Love,
    Charlie x

And she wrote back:

Dear Charlie,
    I am glad you like Max.
    Love,
    Mum x

I hoped Max would become a dad for me. I've seen photographs of my real dad, but that's all. Mum said he was a lovely man but that she was happy just being me and her. Until she met Max. Then it all changed and she wanted to be with him.

So before long, I had to meet Rhino and Germery.

Rhino did an ENORMOUS belch as he came through our front door. Germery followed and gave Mum a look like she was a plate of garlic sprouts.

"Where are your games?" he shouted at me. I had promised Mum I would be nice, so I showed him.

"Her games are rubbish," Germery said when he saw them.

"Jezzie," Max said. "She's called Charlie."

"That's a stupid name," Germery said.

"It's short for Charlotte," Mum said. "I chose it because I liked it."

"Well, you shouldn't have liked it," he said, and pointed his fingers at Mum like he wanted to shoot her.

"Want zappy zappy games," Rhino yelled. "Dad, where's your iPad?"

"At home. We're here to meet Charlie and Sharon, not play on an iPad."

"We're having pizza for lunch," Mum said brightly. "Your dad says you love pizza."

"Don't like pizza," Rhino said, and Germery sneered, "He only likes it when our own mum cooks it."

After lunch (their manners were APPALLING), we went in Max's BMW to the park.

"I hate you," Germery whispered to me.

"I hate you, too," I whispered back. "And you," I added, looking at Rhino, who stuck his tongue out at me.

At the park, a dog came over and Rhino started screaming, so Max picked him up. As he did, the little monster deliberately punched Max's shoulder, really hard.

"Ry, no!" Max said.

FROM THAT MOMENT I decided the baby baboon was going to be called Rhino. Now I needed a name for the big baboon. I didn't have to wait long. A few minutes later, he sneezed a snotty sneeze without covering his mouth with his hand. So from then on, he was Germery.

We went back to our flat and played animal dominoes. It was (of course) another disaster.

"They've not played many games like this," Max said.

"I'd never have guessed," Mum murmured, as Rhino shouted, "Are we going home? It's dead boring here."

Max didn't kiss Mum when they left. He didn't give her a hug either. Or giggle. Or say he'd see us next week.

"Thank you for today," Mum said to me, as Max's BMW drove off. "Was it that awful?"

"They're horrible," I said.

"Shall we make ourselves a cup of tea?" she asked, because Mum and I always drink tea when we're unhappy. I have lots of milk in mine. Mum has a little bit in hers.

"Shall we have a chocolate biscuit as well?" I said, and she nodded.

"I think we both need one," she sighed, and gave me another hug.

*

So one year later we're here, living in Dead End Lane. Max said he would only be one minute sorting Rhino's toilet-paper problem out, but he's upstairs much longer because Germery starts shouting and wants to know when Man U are next on the telly.

"Where were we?" Max says, as he comes back into the living room.

"The Milkshake Detectives logo," I say.

"That's right," he says. "How could I possibly say no? And what would you like on the design?"

"A milkshake, a fingerprint and our name," I say.

"Is it just you and Julia?" he says.

"Agent J," I correct him.

"And are you, by any chance, Agent C?"

I nod and he whispers, "I'll see what I can do, Agent C. Be good doing business with you."

CHAPTER 10

I tell Julia about Max designing a logo for us as we walk to school via the village hall.

"That's great," she says and does a little skip to avoid a cracked paving slab. I do a little skip as well, because I love being a Milkshake Detective.

When we reach the hall we can't see anything bear-like AT ALL.

We look on the way home from school as well. Still nothing.

We look the next day and the day after that and the one after that. Still nothing. At school, everyone is talking about it and inspecting the hall every time they walk past it.

"My mum says the Bear's having a rest,"
William Holdsworth says, but we ignore him
because he doesn't know anything.

On Thursday, Mum is working at the shop
until five o'clock, so I go to Julia's house after
school.

"You'll never guess what," Julia's mum says.
"The Bear left lollipops at the hall for all the
Tumble Tots."

"A lollipop?" Julia and I say together.

"Did the Bear leave a clue as well?" I ask.

"Yup." Tracy nods.

"What is it, then?" Julia asks.

"I wrote it down because I knew you'd want
to know," she says, and hands us a piece of
paper.

Faithful to the very end,

The Bear is searching

for man's best friend.

"Got any ideas about the clue?" Julia says, as
we go up to her bedroom.

"No idea," I say, "but we need to make a list of suspects of who the Bear might be."

Agent J takes out her *Mystery: Solved* notebook. I have mine in my school bag. I also have a pink gel pen Max bought specially for me.

"It has to be someone who likes children," Agent J says, "because so far the Bear has been to our school, the football team and Tumble Tots."

Julia's bedroom is a great place. We rest our notebooks on her window sill and can see the bridge, shop, duck pond, oak tree and most of Peddle High Street. At the moment, Stevie's mum is walking across the grass to the parish notice board by the pond. Stevie isn't with her, so Agent J stays calm – until she gasps and grabs hold of my arm.

"Look at what she's carrying!" she screeches.

In one of Reverend Proctor's hands is an envelope. In the other is a LOLLIPOP!

BAROOPA-DUPA!

Rev Proctor puts the lollipop in her mouth as she pulls a piece of paper out of the envelope and pins it to the board. We watch her sooo carefully. Donny and Ugly watch her as well, then waddle across the grass and sit at her feet. She bends over and talks to them.

"The ducks like her," I say.

"That doesn't mean she's the Bear, though," Agent J says, as Rev Proctor walks back across the grass, towards the church and the vicarage, still sucking her lollipop.

The ducks follow her at first, then flap their wings and glide into the pond.

"There might be a clue in what Stevie's mum's just put on the notice board," I say. Trained detectives automatically know what to do when possible clues need investigating. As one, we stop leaning our elbows on Agent J's window sill and go downstairs and outside.

The notice is about a special Easter service in the church. There are no bears on it but, at the bottom, in really neat handwriting, it says:

Do come and join us,
Lindsay Proctor

"Does the Bear have neat handwriting?" I ask.

"Dunno," Agent J says, and then I nearly explode.

"Look at the colour of the paper! It's BLUE! It's the same colour as the clue on the gnome's fishing rod!"

"Rev Proctor," Agent J squeals, "is our PRIME SUSPECT. We need to think of a reason to go and interview her."

"Why don't we go to the church now and see if there's anything there?" I reply. "She won't realise we're on to her yet. There might be evidence for us to find." (Penelope Pink says evidence is the key to any investigation.)

"Good thinking." Agent J nods.

There is another notice ON BLUE PAPER in the church porch.

Rev Proctor is available for enquiries

5.30 to 6.30

every Wednesday and every Friday,

in the church office.

"Do you think she's inside the church now?" I say, thinking out loud. "If she is, we can't just walk in and stare at her."

"You're right, we can't," Agent J agrees. So we leave the porch and look in the graveyard in case there is anything bear-like there.

Some of the graves are so old the names and dates have worn off. I read Gertrude Miller's gravestone. She died in 1793 aged fifty-four.

Julia is looking at the new gravestones on the other side of the graveyard. "What was your dad's first name?" she calls out.

"Al," I say, and wonder why she's asking. I walk over to where she is. She points at the grave. Someone has put fresh flowers on it. I read the name and go cold all over.

HERE LIES

ALFRED SMITH

AGED 29

TAKEN AWAY TOO SOON

"And what was your dad's second name?" she asks me.

"Smith," I whispered. "It was Smith."

"Whoah," Julia goes.

"It's a funny coincidence, isn't it? This could be your dad. I've worked out the dates. Alfred Smith died just after you were born."

"I don't think it's him," I say. But even as I say the words, my brain is whizzing and I'm thinking, *It MIGHT be him.*

"Your dad's like another mystery," Julia says. "If this isn't him, he's out there somewhere. Have you really never seen him?"

"No," I say, and I wish she would stop talking about him and asking me questions.

"Did your mum used to live here?"

"She's never said so," I whisper. I feel really small and want to tell Julia to SHUT UP. But because I am a Milkshake Detective I have to ask questions and, right now, even though I don't really want to know the answer, I'm asking, *Who put the fresh flowers on the gravestone? And Was it my mum?*

CHAPTER 11

When I wake up, Bertie's nose is digging into my ribs. I wrestle him out, give him a hug and think about the day ahead. We have a day off school because the teachers have a training day.
Germery and Rhino are at Kelly's (yippee!) and they are staying there for the weekend as well (double yippee!). This morning I'm going to the shop with Mum.

PENELOPE PINK: Walking to the shop would be a good time to talk to your mum about your dad.

CHARLIE: I know.

PENELOPE PINK: Good luck!

"How did we end up living in this village?" I ask Mum as we walk towards the bridge.

She wrinkles her nose and says, "The houses were cheap because no one wanted to live here after the dual carriageway was built. So we could afford a house with three bedrooms."

"Have you been to the graveyard yet?" I say, my ears straining to hear her answer.

"You're asking some funny questions this morning," Mum laughs.

"Milkshake Detective work," I reply. I'm thinking about the page in my Mystery: Solved notebook that reads:

The Mystery of My Dad

"But what's the graveyard got to do with working out who the Bear is?"

"Agent J and I are following a lead and we need to know everyone who has visited the graveyard and what they did. Then we can cross them off our list of suspects."

"Ah," Mum says. "Well, yes, I did go there. I took some flowers with Maria."

My heart nearly bursts because I'm beginning

to wonder if that gravestone really *is* my dad's.

"Who were the flowers for?" I ask.

"Maria's nephew is buried there," she replies.

All I can say is, "Oh," but my brain is racing and wondering and I'm not absolutely sure she is telling me the truth. (I don't like that thought, though, because me and Mum are ALWAYS honest with each other. But maybe she thinks I'm not old enough to know about my dad dying, and that's why she's not telling me.)

I am still thinking as we walk down the side of Billy and Maria's house. Supplies for the shop are kept in a massive shed in their back garden. Mum punches what Billy calls 'ET's phone number' into the keypad on the shed door.

"ET5271," Mum whispers as she does it. "Never tell anyone that code."

I smile up at her to let her know I never will.

Inside the shed are shelves and cardboard warehouse boxes: tins of chopped tomatoes are next to the soup; sweetcorn is under the window; toilet rolls, because they are light, are on a high shelf above the door. Mum has carrier bags with her and we fill them with pasta, jars of bolognese sauce and Kit Kats.

"I think that's all Billy said he needed," Mum says. We close the shed door and listen to the lock click into place.

On the other side of the bridge, Donny and Ugly are dragging the plastic pink flamingo with the nasty-looking beak across the road. Billy is standing in his shop doorway laughing at them.

"Aren't you going to get the flamingo back?" Mum calls out as we walk down the ramp.

"No way! Those ducks are feather-covered brutes! I'm not risking my life for a plastic flamingo." We stand next to him until Donny and Ugly dump the bird in the pond, then quack loudly at us.

"Here's a mystery for you and your partner to work out," Billy says to me. "Why are those two ducks so stupid?"

"I don't know," I whisper back.

"Neither do I." He sighs. "But they are funny."

As I check that the shelves are neat and tidy, a man with green shoelaces buys a frozen chicken, garlic bread and a tin of chicken soup. Billy chats about what the man is growing on his allotment. While they talk, I listen and think, *Does the Bear buy frozen chicken and wear green shoelaces?* (I'm not sure.)

A few other people come in to buy newspapers and croissants and toothpaste. I watch them all, but none of them does anything suspicious. Then Stevie's mum, our NUMBER ONE SUSPECT, comes in. My eyes are like magnets attracted to her dark green coat. She takes her purse out of a purple handbag to pay her paper bill. As she does, she drops her purse on the floor. Rev Proctor bends her knees (they creak), picks the purse up and takes some money out of it.

Does the Bear have creaky knees? (I don't know.) Does the Bear have a purple handbag? (No idea!) My eyes never leave Stevie's mum until she walks out of the shop. At the same time, my mobile buzzes and it's Julia. I can go around to hers ALL AFTERNOON. And tonight we are having Chinese takeaway. Today is a beautiful day!

At Julia's, Emily is in her Cinderella dress pretending to make cups of tea. Julia's dad,

Jamie, is about to watch the Arsenal–Chelsea football match on telly. He picks Emily up and dances around the kitchen, singing, "Arsenal, I love you, I'll love you 'til I die, and if you win today, we'll all eat chicken pie."

"Dad, you're SO embarrassing," Julia sighs.

"No, I'm not," he says, pulling a face at her. "But tell me, have the Milkshake Detective super-sleuths worked out who the Bear is yet? I'd be worried if I were him!"

"How do you know it's a he?" Julia says. She is looking at her dad in a very suspicious way.

"It might be a she-Bear," he says quickly, then laughs and says, "Come on, Arsenal. You're going to win today!"

Julia and I decide to make fact-file posters about the Duchess of Cambridge because Julia thinks Kate and Wills are sooo romantic. As we do, Julia says, "I looked on the internet and you can find out about people on gravestones by looking in parish records. They're kept in churches. We could ask Stevie's mum about Alfred Smith *and* interview her about the Bear at the same time."

My heart thumps extra hard because she's

reminded me of what Mum said this morning.

"I'm not sure," I say. "I don't know why Mum wouldn't have told me the truth if he had died."

"Too sad," Julia says, and my tummy feels like a wobbly jelly and I want to stop talking about it. So I start talking about Oliver Garston's latest haircut instead.

An hour later, I roll up my Duchess of Cambridge poster because I want to put it on my bedroom wall. I say goodbye to Julia but instead of going home, I go to Alfred Smith's gravestone. The flowers are drooping a bit today. I wish I was brave like Penelope Pink.

PENELOPE PINK: You are brave, Agent C. Brave enough to find out the truth.

AGENT C: But what if the gravestone *is* my dad's? What if Mum's been keeping loads of secrets from me?

PENELOPE PINK: Only you can know whether the answer is important enough to uncover.

That evening, Max buys crispy duck, king prawn fried rice, Singapore chow mein and prawn crackers. He and Mum giggle as they eat it because Max also bought six red roses and a card with a big red heart on. Then we play Cluedo and Pass the Pigs and I win BOTH games, so I get to choose a DVD. We watch *Up* because I love that film.

Mum sits in the middle of the sofa and holds hands with Max, while I cuddle up to her other side.

When the film finishes, Max says, "Charlie, I have something for you." I wonder (just for a nanosecond) if he and Mum have bought me new curtains. But they haven't, because Max has a piece of paper with the Milkshake Detectives' logo on.

WHOOHOOOPA-LOOPA! It's fantastic. It's got a milkshake and a straw and a cherry that's really a fingerprint and the words THE MILKSHAKE DETECTIVES on it.

"Isn't it great?" Mum says.

"It's . . . " I say. "I *love* it! THANK YOU, MAX!"

"Thought you'd like it," he says. "I've got the file on my laptop, so we can print off as many copies as you want."

"I can't wait to show Agent J," I say, and I want to hug it because it is sooo brilliant.

I put the logo on the arm of the sofa for the rest of the evening, which is a long time, because Man U are on *Match of the Day* and Max thinks I ought to be interested in football. He and I balance bits of popcorn on Mum's knee and flick them towards the telly. Mum hates anything on the carpet so puts a tray in front of her feet. Max and I high-five each other when a piece of popcorn goes in it.

At twenty past ten Max's phone rings. He frowns and flips open his mobile cover.

"It's Kelly." He groans.

"Go on speaker, then, so we can all hear what she's got to say," Mum says.

A soft whisper fills the room above the football commentary Max has turned down. "Hi, darling, it's me."

THAT IS NOT WHAT I EXPECTED KELLY TO

SOUND LIKE! I thought she would have a harsh voice and talk really quickly.

"Are the boys all right?" Max asks.

"That's why I'm ringing."

"What's wrong with them?" Max asks.

"It's Jeremy. He's sneezing and coughing."

"And?" Mum mouths, as her eyes go up to the ceiling then come back down again.

"I really think he would be better back with you," Kelly says.

"Are you scared you might catch what he's got?"

"Darling," Kelly says, "don't get angry with me. You know me well enough. I don't do ill children, and he's got a temperature."

"And if she catches it," Mum whispers, "it will interfere with her plans for next week."

"I think it would be best if you came and collected them."

"What, *now*?"

"Darling, I know," she says. "Do you think I would have phoned if Jeremy hadn't asked for you?"

"Umm," Max goes.

Mum is shaking her head.

"I could possibly collect them a little earlier tomorrow," Max says, "but I'm not coming tonight. Give Jezzie some Calpol."

"Is that the best you can do?"

Now Mum is sooo angry.

"I'll see you tomorrow then," Max says, and presses the end call icon with his index finger.

"Designer mother! That's all she is!" Mum explodes. She bites her lip and stares at Max.

"Please," she says quietly, "turn your mobile off."

Max pauses for a second, then his fingers settle on his mobile screen.

"Thank you," Mum says. "I know that was really hard for you to do."

Max leans in to give Mum a cuddle, then looks at me and says, "It's time for bed, Agent C."

"But I was enjoying the football," I say.

"Time for bed," Mum says. "It's nearly half past ten." All I can think is, *How is it that Kelly and the boys manage to ruin things even when they're not here?*

CHAPTER 12

Max gets up really early to fetch Germery and Rhino. He returns with them as I am about to go out to Julia's.

"They don't seem to be very ill!" Mum says to Max as the boys drag their bags up the stairs.

Max sighs. "Kelly was offered tickets to go to a concert," he says slowly. Mum's mouth drops.

"You have got to be kidding me!" she says.

"No," Max says. I watch as Mum's face freezes then unfreezes.

"How are the detectives today?" Billy asks as Julia and I walk into the village shop. "What's the latest clue?"

"'Faithful to the very end, the Bear is searching for man's best friend'," we say together, then laugh because we have said it so many times and still don't know what it means.

"Would talking to me help you work out what it means?" Billy asks. "We want to know what children like in a milkshake."

"Chopped-up Mars Bars," I say straight away. Mum and I make refrigerator cake with chopped-up Mars Bars and it's yummy.

Behind the counter, Billy bursts out laughing. "If it's got a Mars Bar in it, it could be called Mum's Sheep!"

"Mum's Sheep? Where do you get that from?" Maria says.

"Ma, Mum. Baaaa, sheep." Billy laughs again. "We'll put squirty cream on top to look like a woolly sheep, and a chopped-up Mars Bar in the middle. Do you girls want to try one?"

Now that is a daft question!

As Maria makes two chocolate Mum's Sheep milkshakes, Rob the builder arrives. He is carrying a bucket and a big box with a tap in it.

"You should try one of Maria's bear biscuits,"

he says, as he goes up the stairs. "They're shortbread cut in the shape of bears."

"They can have one of those after I've shown them my latest anti-duck device," Billy says. He's bought a solar-powered bird-scarer that looks like a pair of eyes on a stick. "Those ducks had better realise what a rough, tough and ruthless creature my bird-scarer is!" Billy says. "Go outside and walk in front of it."

We do, and the bird-scarer flashes and makes a howling sound.

"Are you scared of it?" Agent J whispers.

"No," I whisper back, as Billy brings us a tray with the two chocolate Mum's Sheep milkshakes and two shortbread bear biscuits on a plate.

"There you are," he says. "These are on the house as long as you let us know what you think of them."

"Thank you!" we both say. They're the perfect way to start our Milkshake Detective meeting.

I open my bag and take out several sheets of paper with the Milkshake Detectives logo all over them.

"These are for you to cover your notebook

with," I say, and show her my notebook, which Max helped me cover.

"That's brilliant!" Agent J says. She opens her bag and takes out two Alice bands with bears on.

"My dad's bought us these from the shop," she says. "They're to help us think."

"They're nice," I say, slipping one over my hair. Agent J puts hers on as well. "They're like our detective uniforms," I say.

"And," Agent J says, "I've got Dad's first article about the Bear as well. On page five of *The Herald*."

"BEAR" WITNESS TO THIS

For the last four weeks, residents of Peddle-Worth village have been delighted and mystified by someone leaving riddles and anonymous gifts. The latest clue, found with lollipops given to the Tumble Tots meeting in the village hall, was: "Faithful to the very end, the Bear is searching for man's best friend."

Amir Kahn (42), who runs the junior football team which received a new football from the Bear, said, "This is kindness that touches the whole community. Everyone wants to know what the Bear will do next."

"Most people just want to know what the Bear will do next," Agent J says, "but the Milkshake Detectives are trying to work out who the Bear *is*." She straightens her red and white striped jumper and adjusts her Alice band. I glance down the road to see if Stevie or Oli are about to walk past. But the only people I see are two ladies chatting by the parish notice board. "We need more people on our list of suspects," she says. "We've only got Stevie's mum on it at the moment."

Agent J bites off her bear biscuit's head. I bite off my bear biscuit's legs and bottom. The biscuit is sooo yummy.

"Are you going to talk to Stevie's mum about your dad and that gravestone?" she asks.

I take a slurp of my milkshake and drag out a slice of Mars Bar with my spoon. "If I'm wrong, I'll feel stupid," I say.

"But," Julia looks at me like she SO wants me to agree to do this, "it would be the perfect cover to interview our prime suspect, and there'll only be me there."

"Maybe, then," I say. I want to stop talking about it so I pick up my pink gel pen and, at the top of a new page in my notebook, write:

SUSPECTS
1. Rev Proctor

"What about Billy and Maria?" Agent J says. "They know everyone in the village. And they're kind."

"And," I screech, "they buy lollipops from the warehouse and sell them in the shop!"

"You're right, they do!" Agent J says. "They are definitely going on the list." So we write their names down underneath Rev Proctor.

2. Billy Ludolph
3. Maria Ludolph

"What about Mrs Sharp and the teachers at school?" I say.

"No way is it teachers," Agent J says, shaking her head. "None of them live in the village." As she says the word 'village', something flashes in my brain.

"Just had a thought," I say.

"What?"

"We know the Bear hides things. Like the football that was in the hedge but no one saw him or her put it there, and the lollipops that were waiting by the door of the village hall in the morning, but were hidden so we didn't see them."

"Yes . . ."

"Does the Bear go out at night?"

"Woah!" Agent J says. "You are SO right." Then she grins and says, "Why don't we have a Milkshake Detectives sleepover at my house? We can see loads of the village from my bedroom."

I nod excitedly.

"I'll ask my mum," Agent J says. (And we know Tracy will say "yes".)

A few minutes later, William Holdsworth's mum walks down the ramp from the bridge with a sausage dog on a lead trotting next to her.

"Well done, Fluffles," she says to it.

"William Holdsworth has a sausage dog called Fluffles," Agent J whispers, and we both start giggling. I didn't even know he had a dog. I've never seen it before, and the Stinking Baboons have never mentioned it.

"Fluffles," Agent J whispers again.

"Fluffles," I whisper back.

"Do you think she is the Bear?" I whisper.

"Would the Bear have a dog called Fluffles?"

"A dog is a good excuse to walk around the village," I say.

"Good thinking," Agent J whispers as William Holdsworth's mum walks towards us. "We must put her on the suspect list." We both write:

4. William Holdsworth's mum

She is now standing in front of us. "Girls," she says, "could you help me? I don't want to take Fluffles into the shop. Could you watch him if I tie his lead to the back of one of your chairs?"

"OK," Agent J says.

William Holdsworth's mum is suspect number four, so we watch her very closely. Her fingernails are dirty and she is wearing wellies and an old jumper with a hole on her left elbow. She ties Fluffles to Agent J's chair then goes into the shop.

The first thing Fluffles does is try to escape by heading back towards the bridge.

"Fluffles, come here!" Agent J says as Billy's bird-scarer springs into life, letting off a bloodcurdling howl, bright lights flashing out of its eyes.

Fluffles is not a brave dog. He dives under the table where he balances on four trembling little legs.

"He's so scared," Agent J says.

"He's going to be even more scared in a minute," I say, pointing at two ducks waddling as fast as they can towards the bird- (and dog-) scarer. They honk at it, which makes Fluffles whimper even more. Then they grab hold of its base with their beaks, topple it over and drag it to join the pink plastic flamingo in the bottom of the pond across the road.

Agent J and I stroke Fluffles's ears. "Those nasty ducky-ducks have gone," Agent J says to him.

He nuzzles the side of his head into the palm of her hand.

"He's very sweet," I say, and we stay there talking to him until William Holdsworth's mum comes out of the shop.

"How's Fluffles been?" she says.

"He doesn't like Billy's bird-scarer. Or the ducks," I say.

"I thought a dog was supposed to be a man's best friend and protect him," she says with a laugh as she unties Fluffles' lead.

Agent J and I do not say a word. We just smile and nod and look at the bag she is carrying as she walks to the top of the ramp and on to the bridge. Then Agent J whispers, "Man's best friend!"

And I whisper back, "Man's best friend! That's exactly what it said on the Bear clue! Let's move her up our list of suspects to being equal first with Rev Proctor."

I take out my invisible ink pen that was part of my *Mystery: Solved* detective kit.

"We should write our suspects' names in invisible ink in case someone finds our notebooks and reads who we think it is," I continue.

1. Rev Proctor and William Holdsworth's mum
2. Billy Ludolph
3. Maria Ludolph

The writing glistens on the page, then disappears as the ink dries and fades into being invisible.

"Let's put Mr Kahn on as well," I say. "He was there when Arthur Rivers found the football and might have hidden it in the hedge before football practice started."

"OK," Agent J agrees. "Now we have FIVE suspects and know that the next clue is going to lead us to a dog."

"That's a good morning's work," I say. "AND we got a free milkshake and biscuit."

"Agent C," Agent J says, "we are going to crack this case." (Sabrina Scarlett says that in episode five of series one).

But where is the dog?

We tell Billy and Maria we love Mum's Sheep milkshakes. We also tell them about the bird-scarer. Then we check with Mum that it's OK for me to go to Julia's for a sleepover.

"Is that tonight?" she says, and we nod. "Can you be home in time for lunch tomorrow?" We nod again.

Julia and I head to my house to pack my bag.

While I find my sleeping bag, teddy bear, PJs and toothbrush, Julia kneels on my bed, pushes the Peppa Pig curtains (SO embarrassing) out of the way, and looks down at the garden.

"Your little brothers are building something out of boxes," she says.

Straight away I say, "Those two stinky-poos are not my brothers! They're pains in the neck." I kneel next to her to see what they're doing. Rhino is trying to balance a big box on top of a small one. It keeps toppling over, so Germery helps him swap boxes so that the big one is underneath. As we watch, Max walks down the garden. The boys throw their arms around his legs to try to stop him walking. Then all three put cardboard boxes over their heads and walk around the garden with their arms held out in front of them.

"I think they're pretending to be bears," Julia says. "They're quite sweet, aren't they?"

"They're not!" I say. "They're numpty-dumpties!"

Tracy puts a blow-up mattress on the floor in Julia's bedroom and we put our supply of chocolate biscuits, jelly babies and lemonade on the window sill next to our notebooks and pens. When we've closed the curtains (they have tiny fairies sliding down rainbows on them and are sooo beautiful), we pop our heads underneath them so that we can see out. Julia's panda and Bertie sit on the window sill as well. Then we wait. And wait. Eight people walk over the bridge but none of them carry anything except handbags, and none of them looks like a Bear.

"Maybe the Bear's not doing anything tonight," I say.

"The Bear will be out," Agent J says. "I just KNOW he will be."

"I so want to win that prize," I say.

"But we don't know what the prize is yet," Agent J says.

"It could be a Bear onesie," I say.

"Too obvious and it's not unique," Agent J says. "I think it's a year's supply of gummy bears."

"That's not unique either," I say. Thinking what the prize could be is a mystery in itself!

We've just finished the last jelly baby, and Agent J is about to nip to the loo for the second time, when a shadowy figure lumbers across the bridge from Worth and pauses by the lamp post at the bottom of the ramp in Peddle.

FLUFFLING-FLOOFLEPOTS! IT'S THE BEAR! It's someone wearing a bear costume, with a little tail and sticking-up ears.

"I think the Bear is a woman," I say.

"I was thinking the same," Agent J says.

"She's not carrying anything," I whisper, as the Bear hurries down Peddle High Street towards the playing field and the church.

Then Julia's hand shoots across and jolts my elbow. "Look at the ducks," she squeals.

Two shadowy duck-shapes are shuffling over the grass towards the Bear, who stops and waits for them to reach her. She bends over and talks to them and their heads nod up and down like they are agreeing with what she is saying. Then they waddle back to the pond.

"Do you remember," I ask, "the ducks said hello to Stevie's mum when she stuck that notice about the Easter service on the parish board?"

"They did, didn't they?" Agent J says. "That is evidence. But do we know if anyone else likes them?"

"Billy and Maria save the out-of-date bread for them," I say.

We look at our list of suspects. Mr Kahn and Billy are men. That leaves Rev Proctor, William Holdsworth's mum and Maria. We know that Rev Proctor and Maria like the ducks.

"But we don't know if William Holdsworth's mum does," Agent J says.

"Fluffles doesn't," I say.

"So I don't think William Holdsworth's mum does either," Agent J says.

We wait for the Bear to return. We wait. And we wait. The church clock strikes midnight. We've eaten all our food and drunk most of the lemonade. I am sooo tried and I need to go to the loo. I think Agent J is tired as well, because when I suggest going to sleep she agrees straight away.

But it is odd that the Bear never came back.

CHAPTER 13

"I think we should watch the ducks because we know they like the Bear," Julia says as we finish our breakfast. We go outside and sit on the bench watching Donny and Ugly up-end themselves, run their beaks through their feathers and flap in and out of the reeds at the side of the pond.

The church service finishes and people leave the churchyard. Donny and Ugly ignore everyone UNTIL WILLIAM HOLDSWORTH'S MOTHER WALKS BY! When she does, Donny quacks three times, then both ducks charge across the grass towards her.

"Are you seeing what I am seeing?" Agent J whispers.

"I am," I whisper back. "We were wrong! They do like her!"

The ducks follow William Holdsworth's mum along Peddle High Street, past the shop, up Peddle ramp and over the bridge.

"Maria's coming up over Worth ramp now!" Agent J says. We watch them meet in the middle of the bridge and start talking to each other.

"Two of our prime suspects," I say. "In broad daylight."

Highly trained agents do not need to discuss what to do when two suspects meet. We slide off the bench and walk around Peddle ramp, our ears straining to hear what William Holdsworth's mum and Maria are saying to each other.

"It's not looking good," Maria says.

"I'll keep an eye on it," William Holdsworth's mum says. "What's the time limit?"

"Not much longer," Maria says, and then sees us and smiles. "And what are you two doing this morning?" she asks.

"Been for a sleepover at Julia's," I say.

"Bet you didn't get much sleep then," William Holdsworth's mum laughs.

"I had a bad night," Maria says and yawns. "There was a cat meowing in our garden just after midnight. Woke me up."

"Cats are so annoying," William Holdsworth's mum says. "Give me a dog any day."

Agent J and I smile at them, then carry on walking.

"Did you notice how Maria wanted us to know she was in bed at midnight?" Agent J says. "WHICH PROBABLY MEANS SHE WASN'T! Maria is my top suspect at the moment."

"I still think it's William Holdsworth's mum, or Stevie's," I say. This is sooo brilliant!

Then it's not because Agent J looks at me and says, "Charlie, we *have* to interview Stevie's mum. Asking about that grave is the most perfect excuse. Are we going to do it?"

I pause.

"If you don't do it, you might never find out," Julia says.

*

I turn into Dead End Lane carrying my sleeping bag in one hand and a carrier bag in the other. The baboons are riding up and down the pavement making bear noises. The Milkshake Detective Agency is following up real leads about who the Bear is. Rhino and Germery are just making a lot of noise and being pathetic.

"You're a gwizzly bear!" Rhino yells and cycles so fast down the pavement I have to jump out of the way.

"Oy! You nearly ran into me," I shout at him.

"That's what bear hunters do," Germery shouts back. "And you're a nasty grizzly and I'm coming to get you."

Max's BMW is parked outside our house. I dodge around the side of it. Germery swerves at the very last second. He swerves so late that his pedal scrapes along the BMW. There's now a scratch the size of a giant caterpillar on Max's precious car.

I go straight into our kitchen.

"Had a good time?" Mum asks.

"Yup. We have a list of suspects!" I tell her. Then I say, "Germery's just run his bike into Max's car."

Mum looks up from the gravy she is making. Max looks up from putting knives and forks on the table. His nose flares out (his nostrils do that when he is super-cross). I go into the living room as Max storms out of the back door.

A minute later Max and Germery walk up the path.

"You're going to buy a can of special car paint," Max says as they come into the kitchen. "Your mother gives you loads of pocket money, so you can use some of that."

Germery is getting a telling off from Max! Mind you, all Germery will do is go upstairs and phone Kelly on the blue mobile and she'll give him extra money next time she sees him.

That night there's a note in the fairy box.

Dear Charlie,
    How many people have you got on your list of suspects now?
    Love,
    Mum xxxxxxx

I leave a note in reply:

Dear Mummy,
    We have three prime suspects
and two others but I am not telling
you who they are!
    Charlie xxxxxx

CHAPTER 14

After school on Wednesday, I go to Julia's house.
I have a black skirt and a white shirt in my bag,
because I want to look like Penelope Pink did
when she interviewed the zookeeper in episode
six of series one. Agent J changes into smart
clothes as well. She puts lipstick on and offers it
to me. I shake my head because Mum doesn't
want me wearing make-up until I am at senior
school. At exactly half past four we leave Julia's
house and walk to the church.

"We'll only talk about your dad for a
minute," Julia says. "Then we'll get on to the
Bear."

I wish my heart would stop thumping.

Stevie's mum's office is built on to the side of the church. Julia presses the bell and we wait until Rev Proctor opens the door.

"Hello, girls," she says, and smiles like she's really pleased to see us. "Is it me you want to see?" And we nod (though I think Julia would love to see Stevie). "Come in then," she says, and leads us to a room with a big desk, lots of books and four comfy chairs. "Do sit down."

My legs only just touch the floor when I sit back in the chair, so I shuffle forwards and perch on the edge of the cushion while Julia stares at a photograph of Stevie dressed in a waistcoat and bow tie.

"How can I help?" Rev Proctor says.

"I'm looking for my dad," I say, and then I don't know what to say next. Rev Proctor's head tilts slightly to the left as she says, "Would you like to tell me what you already know about him?"

"His name was Al Smith," I say. "I've only ever seen pictures of him. You've got an Alfred Smith in the graveyard and he died at about the same time my mum says my dad left us and ... "

I can't get any more words out because I've always imagined my dad would come back one day. But if the Alfred Smith in the graveyard *is* my dad, then he's never coming back and all the things I've imagined my dad and I would do together were just a stupid waste of time. So I say, "Someone's put fresh flowers on his grave and my mum's been to the graveyard, with Maria, and put flowers on a grave. And I thought ... "

"Charlie," Rev Proctor says, and her voice is very gentle, "Alfred Smith was Maria's nephew. He grew up in Peddle-Worth and had a long illness before he died. I'm pretty sure Alf wasn't your dad."

I stare at her and my eyes are watering tears all down my cheeks. Julia squeezes on to the seat next to me and puts her arm around me. Rev Proctor pulls a tissue out of a box on her desk.

"Did you want Alfred Smith to be your dad?" she asks.

"I just want a dad," I blurt out.

"What about Max?" Rev Proctor says. "Isn't he like a dad?"

"He's Jeremy's and Ryan's dad," I whisper,

and am glad I remember to get their names right. "He's not *my* dad. He's theirs."

The clock on the shelf ticks as we sit there and no one says anything for a few moments until Julia says, "Do you know what the Bear's going to do next?" And I swivel my eyes towards her because I hadn't expected her to ask that sort of question.

"Have you worked out the latest clue about the best friend?" Rev Proctor asks. She is talking to Agent J and not to me.

"We think it's to do with a dog," Agent J says.

"When you leave," Rev Proctor says, "have a look in the graveyard."

"So you know something?" Agent J almost gasps.

"I'm not saying anything except *look in the graveyard*." The clock is still ticking. I want to leave, but Stevie's mum says, "Charlie, you must tell your mum about wanting to know more about your dad."

Before this afternoon I didn't want to tell Mum at all. But now I'm thinking maybe I ought to. So I nod and say I will. Julia takes the tissue out of my hand and moves across the room to put it in the bin (which is under the shelf where the photograph of Stevie is).

"If you ever want to talk more about this, do come and see me," Rev Proctor says as we leave.

"Thank you," I whisper.

Julia and I walk down the path from Rev Proctor's office to the graveyard. We go to Alfred Smith's gravestone. The flowers on his grave are completely dried up now. Mum did tell me the truth. My dad left when I was too little to remember. He just went and never came back.

I don't have a dad.

I never had one who stayed long enough to get to know me.

It was always just me and Mum.

Until Max turned up with Rhino and Germery.

"We must look at every grave," Agent J says. "There might be one with a picture of a dog on it."

We walk around the graveyard looking at every grave, until we come to the war memorial. There, we both stop. The war memorial is a statue of a soldier with a dog at his feet.

The dog has a brown ribbon around his neck with something on blue paper hanging from it.

"The Bear must have been coming here on Saturday night," I say.

"The Bear is not Stevie's mum then," Agent J says, "unless she went somewhere first, then came back to the graveyard in her bear costume."

"But she lives next to the church and the graveyard. Why would she bother to dress up as a bear and walk around the village at midnight?" I say. "She could come here in one minute, then go back to bed."

"So it can't be Rev Proctor," Agent J says. "Better cross her off our list."

"It has to be Maria or William Holdsworth's mum." And I'm a little bit sad about that, because I like Stevie's mum.

The clue around the dog's neck says:

Seeds are sown,

Vegetables grown,

Fruit shoots,

Wear your boots.

"That's the allotments," I say. "Shall we go there now?"

"No," Agent J says. "The Bear won't do anything until she knows lots of other people have been to the graveyard. I think Stevie's mum only told us about it because no one else has found it yet."

"Woah!" I say. "If that's why she told us, but she isn't the Bear, does that mean there are *several* adults working on the Bear Hunt, but only one of them dresses up?"

A robin perches on a gravestone and bobs his tail. Agent J and I think really hard.

"I think you could be right," Agent J says. "The Milkshake Detectives will have to keep sniffing out the evidence."

CHAPTER 15

Agent J and I check the allotments each day. Nothing is ever there. Then Agent J says she wants to check something else. At school, she asks William Holdsworth, "Does your mum ever do any sewing?"

He looks at her and screws his face up. He has a blob of toothpaste spit on his school sweatshirt that moves up and down when he breathes. "No," he says.

"She hasn't made a bear costume then," Agent J whispers to me.

"But Maria sews," I suddenly remember. "She made bear puppets to sell at the shop. I saw them lying on the kitchen table, half finished."

"*She* could have made the bear costume then," Agent J says.

I nod, because she could have done. Though the Bear could also have bought a onesie from a shop.

"Mum," I say, as she and I put chocolate drops on top of our latest batch of cupcakes, "I've been thinking about my dad."

"Your dad?" she says, and there's surprise in her voice.

"I want to get in touch with him."

"Er, Charlie. I'm not sure that's such a good idea. He didn't want ... " She stops herself.

"Didn't want what, Mum?"

"Your dad wasn't ready to settle down with a family," she says quickly.

"I still want to meet him," I whisper, but my voice is a little bit trembly. "Do you have an address? I want to write to him."

"Charlie, he left nine years ago. He went travelling. He could be anywhere."

"But he must live somewhere," I say.

"The only address I have is the house he rented." Mum picks up a chocolate drop and cuts it in half with her sharp knife. "Charlie, please don't get your hopes up."

She gives me my dad's last known address. I write it down in invisible ink in the back of my notebook. Not even Agent J knows it is there.

I take it with me the following Saturday when I go to the shop with Mum.

"Going to help me unpack this then?" Billy says. He has a huge cardboard box. "It's my latest way of protecting customers from vicious ducks." This time he has bought twelve garden gnomes with daft grins on their faces and wheelbarrows in front of them.

"These are hard-core warrior gnomes," he says. "Donny and Ugly will be terrified of them."

"Will they?" I ask.

Billy nods. "Ducks hate wheelbarrows," he says, solemnly. (Do they?)

We position the gnomes in front of the tables and all the time I am thinking, *The Bear stuck a garden gnome with a fishing rod in the old oak tree for the first clue. Agent J and I thought the Bear was female. BUT MAYBE THE BEAR IS BILLY, wearing a bear costume that Maria made for him!*

Once the hard-core warrior garden gnomes are settled and protecting the shop, Billy and I go inside.

"Had any more ideas for milkshakes?" he asks, and actually I have. I tell him and he laughs.

"That is clever," he says. "Shall I make one for you?" That is a daft question!

"Would you like a banana, strawberry or chocolate?" he asks. (That is a daft question, too.)

"Chocolate, please," I say.

"What fruit would you like? We have strawberries, cherries and blueberries today."

I choose cherry and watch Billy mix the powder, ice cream and milk in the blender, whizz it around then empty the contents into a tall glass. He squirts cream on top and lines five Smarties next to each other with a cherry at the top.

"And that is a Smart Tie milkshake." He grins as he passes it to me.

I say, "You could use the tube of chocolate syrup and draw two triangles on either side of the cherry so it looks like a shirt collar."

"Clever thinking!" Billy says, picking up the syrup. "Brilliant!" he says a few seconds later. "I really like that."

I drink my milkshake (it's yummy, but not as yummy as a Mum's Sheep milkshake) sitting on the stairs inside the shop because Hollie's nan and someone I don't know are at the table in the shop and it's cold outside. I only go up to the fifth step because Billy has said NO ONE whatsoever, except Rob the builder and Maria and Billy, are going up to the new café until it is finished.

A man wearing a green jacket buys a birthday card and two litres of milk. Mr Kahn comes in with his little boy and buys toilet rolls, a tin of chopped tomatoes and a magazine. I watch him really carefully but he does NOTHING WHATSOEVER that is bear-like (which is sooo disappointing).

And then the door flies open and Julia rushes in. She knows where I am because I texted her.

"Look at this!" she says and I squeeze over so she can join me sitting on the fifth step. She is holding a copy of *The Herald*. Her dad's had another article published AND WE ARE IN IT!

105

PEDDLE-WORTH BEARS FRUIT

Residents of Peddle-Worth village continue to be excited by the Bear's hunt for mystery clues. Last week's clue was difficult and not many children worked out that they had to find the dog at the World War One memorial in the church graveyard. Two children who did find it were Charlie Smith (9) and Julia Sopton (10). They call themselves the Milkshake Detectives and the budding super-sleuths are now working on the next clue, which is:

Seeds are sown, Vegetables grown, Fruit shoots, Wear your boots. Rev Proctor (43) said, "It is lovely how children are working together to solve the clues and the Bear certainly gives everyone something to talk about." Billy Ludolph (61) who owns the village shop, said, "This village was split in two when the dual carriageway was built four years ago. It is now coming together to solve the clues and that can only be good for the community."

"Wow!" I say. "The Milkshake Detectives are famous!"

"Dad bought two newspapers," Agent J says, taking a second copy out of her bag, "so we can each stick the article in our notebooks." We balance them on our laps and take it in turns to use Agent J's scissors and glue; but I keep reading the lines where the Milkshake Detectives and our names are mentioned and thinking, *Maybe my real dad will read it*. And I'd love him to. I'd love him to come and find me as well.

As Agent J puts her glue stick away, Oliver Garston and his mum walk into the shop.

"Hello," he says, and smiles at us.

"Hi," I say back.

"Hi . . . " Julia echoes and then stops. Her cheeks look like bright red Smarties.

"You *do* fancy him," I whisper as Oliver's mum opens the sliding door at the top of the freezer.

"No, I don't," Agent J whispers back, but her eyes never leave Oli's curly brown hair. *Giraffes don't have long necks, either.*

"I think we need to put Billy back on our list of suspects," I whisper, as Oli and his mum leave the shop and Agent J can concentrate on being a Milkshake Detective once more.

"Why?" she says.

"Because of the gnomes he's put outside the shop. I know his gnomes have wheelbarrows and the one in the tree with the first clue had a fishing rod, but I still think he likes gnomes."

Agent J nods and agrees with me.

"Time for another new list?" she giggles. We have sooo many lists it's getting ridiculous!

"Good idea," I say, taking out my invisible writing pen. "Penelope Pink used a code where letters were two further on in the alphabet. So A was C, B was D and so on." That's the code we use, and underneath we write down our evidence as well (not in code; that would take FOR EVER to work out).

1. Yknnkco Janfuyqtvj'u owo
   Female.
   She said "Man's best friend".
   Donny and Ugly follow her.
   Fluffles is an excuse to walk
     around the village.
   BUT – she doesn't sew (she hasn't
     made a bear costume).

"Does she ever go to the allotment?" Agent J asks.

"Don't know," I say. "We'll have to ask William."

"He's useless," Agent J says.

"But his mum is our PRIME SUSPECT," I say. "He's still useless."

2. Octkc Nwfqnrj
   Female.
   Likes the ducks (gives them stale bread).
   Sells lollipops.
   She sews (so could make a bear costume).
   BUT – she said she was in bed when we saw the Bear. (Do we believe her? NO!)

"And," I suddenly whisper, "Maria and Billy are making money out of the Bear by selling bear biscuits and bear masks and all the other bear stuff they've got in the shop."

"You're right," Agent J says. "Add that to the list. For Billy as well." So we write:

Makes money out of the Bear.

"I think that makes her an equal prime suspect," I say, and Agent J agrees.

109

3. Tgx Rtqevqt
   Female.
   Eats lollipops.
   Ducks like her.
   Uses blue paper.
   Knew about the dog clue in the
      graveyard.
   BUT - did not need to walk
      round the village to reach
      the graveyard.

"Is she a prime suspect as well?" I ask.

"No," Agent J says. "She is an ordinary suspect."

4. Dknna Nwfqnrj
   Sells lollipops.
   Buys gnomes.
   Makes money out of the Bear.
   Has a wife who sews (she could
      make him a costume).

"The ducks love him," I say. "They come to visit him all the time."

"And he tries to get rid of them!" Agent J says back, "In case they blow his cover."

So we add:

> Ducks love him.
> BUT – he wants us to think they
>   don't.
> AND – he is not female.

"I think he is an ordinary suspect as well," Agent J whispers.

> 5. Ot Mcjp
>   Was there when the football was
>   found.
>   BUT – he is not female.

"He's not really a suspect, is he?" I say.

"No, he's not," Agent J says. "Let's cross him off." She shines her ultra-violet light at the blank page to make the writing appear so she can see to cross him off.

"Is there anyone else we could add?" I say.

Agent J frowns as she thinks. "If the Bear is Billy or Maria," she says, "it could be your mum, as well!"

"My mum?" I echo. I have never, ever

thought of that. "She's not said anything about being the Bear."

"She wouldn't, would she?" Agent J says.

She's right, Mum wouldn't.

So in place of Mr Kahn at number five, we write:

5. Ejctnkg'u owo
   Female.
   Works in the shop.

"Shall we check the allotments again?" Agent J says, and I know why she wants to. We walk over the bridge and turn left and then slow down as we pass the house with the wooden owl sitting by the front door.

"Oli's not there," I say. He never is. (I think he sees her walking towards his house and hides.)

At the allotments the gate's still there with a padlock on. The railings haven't changed, and neither have the sheds or plants or vegetables.

"I think the Bear will hang something from this gate," Agent J says. "We must check it all the time if we are to find the next clue before anyone else."

"That means we'll have to keep walking past Oli's house," I say, and giggle as she says, "Oh, yes, so it does," in a surprised sort of way.

Julia wants to try the Smart Tie milkshake, so we go back to the shop (slowing down past Oli's house, of course) and sit outside. Shannon from Year Three and her dad are there drinking strawberry Mum's Sheep milkshakes and eating bear biscuits. Shannon has a bear puppet on her hand that she has bought from the shop.

Before long, Donny and Ugly's beady little eyes spot us.

"Looks like the ducks want some of your biscuit," Shannon's dad says with a laugh as they waddle towards us. But those ducks aren't interested in bear biscuits. They want to take out the hard-core warrior gnomes. Ugly knocks two of them over with one swift jerk of her beak and Donny head-butts another one, then grabs the wheelbarrow in his beak.

Julia goes all dramatic and jumps on her chair. "They're going to bite me!" she screams.

I stand on my chair as well and we hug each other like that will stop the ducks sucking blood out of our toes. Shannon jumps on to her dad's lap.

"Those gnomes are rubbish at protecting us!" Julia cries.

"But I'm not," Billy's voice says. We look at the shop doorway and he and Rob are holding SuperSoaka water pistols.

"Do you need saving by knights in shining armour?" Rob laughs.

"Yes, we do," Julia wails in a pathetic voice as Billy aims just below Donny's big, fat bottom.

SPLOOOSH!

"This is what I call Chinese takeawaying the ducks!" he says.

"Wow!" Shannon says as Donny honks loudly, spreads his wings, races across the road and launches himself back on to the pond.

"That was impressive!" Shannon's dad laughs as Rob squirts water just below Ugly's bottom. She's not like Donny and hisses at him. Rob squirts the ground again and this time Ugly waddles across the road, then sits on the grass.

"That one's a troublemaker," Billy says. "She leads Donny astray. Now, would my valued customers like another milkshake to make up for the disturbance those ducks have caused?"

"Yes, please," we all say, and I am thinking, *Would the Bear shoot water at ducks?*

CHAPTER 16

On the way back to 3, Dead End Lane I make up my mind to do something. Something really important. Max is in the house on his own. I ask him to print me off a sheet of paper with the Milkshake Detectives logo at the top.

"What's it for?" he asks.

"A letter," I say. "Milkshake Detective business."

"Would you like me to help you?" Max says, and it's like he knows what I am going to do. "Your mum said you were asking about your dad. Are you writing to who I think you're writing to?"

My head gives a little nod and I tell him

about finding the gravestone and going to see Stevie's mum and how I really, REALLY want to find out about my dad.

"Charlie, are you sure you want to do this?" he asks me.

"I really do," I say. "But I don't want my dad to know it's from me. So I'm going to write as if I'm a proper detective."

"OK," he says and together we write:

The Milkshake Detective Agency
3, Dead End Lane
Peddle-Worth
PW3 4MD

23rd April

Dear Mr Smith,
The Milkshake Detective Agency specialises in helping connect children with their parents. We are working with a girl called Charlotte

*Elizabeth Smith and have reason to believe you
are her father. She would very much like to hear
from you.*

*Please reply using the stamped addressed
envelope so that, if possible, we can arrange for
you to meet her.*

Yours sincerely,

I pause when I am about to write my name. I
don't want to sign Charlie Smith because my
dad might guess it's me and sometimes
(because this happened in *Mystery: Solved*),
people don't want to be reunited with their
families.

"You could use my surname if you wanted,"
Max says. "You could call yourself Lottie
Warburton. How does that sound?"

It sounds all right. So that is how I sign
myself:

Lottie Warburton

That night I lie in bed and cuddle Bertie. I
imagine what my dad's like. I often do that.
Tonight I give him short black hair and a kind

face. He holds his arms out for me to run into and buys me some new curtains to make up for all the birthdays he's forgotten. Then he takes me to an expensive Italian restaurant and says I can visit him every other weekend and what a clever way it was to find him by using the Milkshake Detective Agency.

CHAPTER 17

Being in the shop is even more important now as Maria, Billy and MY MUM (I still don't think it is her) are there. It's great because the Easter holidays have arrived, the baboons are at Kelly's for a few days, and we have two whole weeks off school. Julia and I keep checking the allotments (and Oli Garston's house). Nothing is ever there, though.

On Monday afternoon Maria says, "I'm making biscuits. Want to come and help me?" Of course I go. This could be a Milkshake Detective breakthrough.

"Your mum says you have a list of Bear

suspects," Maria says as we weigh the sugar and margarine. "Who's on it?"

WOAH! I didn't expect that question.

"It's a secret," I say.

"Billy and I think the Bear is someone who has children," she says, "because the Bear is a fun sort of thing to do."

Now that is something Agent J and I haven't thought about. From our list of possible suspects, that would be William Holdsworth's mum, Stevie Proctor's mum and my mum. It would also be Mr Kahn (he's going to have to go back on the suspect list), because he has a little boy who goes to Tumble Tots (which is where the lollipops were).

"That's interesting," I say. I sooo need to talk to Agent J!

We are about to start making a second batch of biscuits when Billy phones from the shop. He's sold the last bottle of olive oil and needs some more.

"Could you take it?" Maria asks me. We go to the shed and she presses ET's phone number (ET5271) into the keypad. She lets me watch her punch the number in because she knows I will never tell it to anyone.

As I walk over the bridge with three bottles of olive oil, Donny waddles towards me.

"And what are you doing today?" I ask him. He ignores me and sticks his head through the railings. He's going to honk at the cars below. I expect Ugly will join him soon.

"Thank you," Billy says, as I put the bottles on the shelf next to the vinegar and tomato ketchup. "Are you doing any Milkshake Detective business today, or is it your day off?"

"My partner isn't here," I say. "I'm having a day off."

"Oh." He smiles. "Just checking you weren't secretly interviewing my wife for information."

Actually, it was the other way round, and one of our prime suspects said something that was useful to us!

Later in the week, Max goes to town. He takes Julia and me with him as he's going to drop us off at the swimming pool. We sit in the back of his BMW while he sings along to his country and western music and then we get the giggles because he is sooo out of tune.

I swim three lengths in a row. I've never swum that far before. Julia dives in at the deep end and has never done that before either. But the best bit of the day is when Max is driving us home. He says, "Charlie, I've got the measurements of your bedroom window in my pocket. Shall we see if we can find some new curtains for you?"

ZOOPER-WHOOPERS!

We stop at the big outlet store. Julia helps me choose blue curtains with shapes like magnifying glasses on them. Max looks at the price and nearly collapses on the floor.

"Are they too much?" I ask.

He pauses then clears his throat. "Charlie," he says, "if they're the ones you really want, I'll buy them!"

I'VE GOT SOME PROPER, GROWN-UP CURTAINS!

I leave a note in the fairy box:

Dear Mummy,
    Thank you for my curtains. I love them!
    Love,
    Charlie xxxxxx

She writes back:

Dear Charlie,
    Thank you for being so patient.
Love you,
Mum xxxxxxx

My new curtains look brilliant and on Thursday
I stay in my bedroom just to be near them! I
start making a fluffy felt owl from a kit Maria
gave me.

At half past ten, the front doorbell rings. The
stinkers are back from Kelly's. I hear Mum open
the front door.

"Hello! What's in the box?" she says.

"A telly for our bedroom," Germery answers.

"A what?" I can tell Mum is really, REALLY
ANGRY but trying not to show it.

"A telly," Germery repeats and his voice is
louder. "Our mum bought it for us to watch in
our bedroom."

"She didn't ask me or your father about it."

"She didn't have to," he says.

"That telly stays on the doorstep until I have

spoken to your dad," Mum says. "Now take your bags upstairs. Did your mum wash your clothes while you were away?"

"No," Germery says. "She said you could do it."

When I go downstairs, the boys are on their PlayStation and Mum is talking to Max on the phone. She won't want me to disturb her, so I write a note:

Gone to Julia's. Be back for supper.

Julia and I make up a bear rhyme to use with her new skipping rope that has bear handles. At school, Hollie and Gemma are always making bear rhymes up. Ours goes like this:

Bears go up and bears go down
And sometimes they ride into town.
Their feet are flat, their tails are long
And when they're bored they sing a song.

We play with the skipping rope for a while, then Julia has an idea for a new milkshake, so we

run to the shop. Maria is making banana and
strawberry Mum's Sheep milkshakes for Freya,
who's in Year Four and her older sister, whose
name I don't know.

"And what can I do for you two?" Maria says,
when Freya and her sister go outside.

"I've had a bear milkshake idea," Julia says.
"Put a shortbread biscuit in the milkshake and
it'll look like the bear is swimming. You could
call it a Swim Bear milkshake."

"I like the idea," Maria says, "but I'm not sure
about the name. Let me think about that one."
Then she leans across the counter. There are
three other people in the shop. She checks that
none of them is listening. "Freya and Millie said
they saw the Bear yesterday afternoon," she
whispers.

"They saw her?" Julia whispers back.
"Where?"

"Walking down Chippers Lane. In broad
daylight."

"When?"

"In the morning."

That is so unfair! THE BEAR SHOULD HAVE
BEEN WHERE WE WERE!

The Milkshake Detectives know what to do when someone has seen the Bear. We thank Maria for the tip-off, walk through the shop door and sit down opposite Freya and her big sister, whose name I now know is Millie.

"Did you see the Bear?" Agent J asks them, and both of them nod. "Tell us what you saw," she says.

"He started running when he saw us," Freya says. "He was dead fast, so we didn't bother chasing him."

"Shhhush!" Millie says and prods her. "Don't tell them what we saw."

"What do you think the prize is going to be?" Agent J says to try and get them to tell us more.

"A huge teddy bear," Freya says.

"A box of chocolate bears," Millie says.

"We think the prize might be a trip to see a bear," I say.

"There are bears at the zoo," Freya says. "Our mum took us there on Monday and we went in this water cave thing and the polar bears were swimming over the top of us."

"And you got scared, didn't you?" Millie says.

"I didn't!"

Going to the zoo sounds like a nice prize, but it's not unique. Anyone can go to the zoo if they have a ticket.

We chat a bit about what we've been doing in the holidays, then Agent J and I get up to go.

"They thought the Bear was male," Agent J says, as we walk under the oak tree towards the bench by the pond.

"And he can run fast," I add. "But he goes out in the daytime."

"That has to be Mr Kahn then," Agent J says.

I nod and say, "My mum can't run fast and she and Maria went to the warehouse yesterday afternoon. So the Bear is definitely not either of them."

"Not another list!" Agent J says.

"Yup!" I say. "Cross off Maria and my mum. Add Mr Kahn. Keep on Billy. Our number one, top, PRIME SUSPECT is still WILLIAM HOLDSWORTH'S MUM."

"Agreed," Agent J says.

The box with the telly is no longer on the steps by the front door. Max is setting up a television in the living room next to our old one.

"This is for the boys to play their PlayStation on," he says. "Because it's not going upstairs."

Germery's eyes are red. He has been crying.

After supper, Rhino and Germery go outside and Mum and I play a game of Pass the Pigs.

"Are you going to be upset if your dad doesn't write back?" Mum asks, as I shake the pigs in my cupped hands.

"No," I say, because that is what she wants me to say.

"You're very precious to me, and to Max," she says. I throw the two pigs and they land on their feet. "That's twenty points," Mum says, and writes my score down.

When she throws the pigs they land facing each other. "That's zero," Mum says and sighs. "Only I don't want you getting hurt."

I wish she would stop talking about my dad. I just want to meet him, to see what he looks like and hear how he talks (and hope that he wants to see me again). After all, he is my real dad.

We finish playing Pass the Pigs. Mum wins by eleven points. And then Max's voice fills the room, shouting at the boys.

"What have they done now?" Mum sighs.

It's something to do with the can of spray paint Germery bought for Max's car.

It should only ever be used by Max, and no one else.

And only on a car.

And certainly not ever, EVER on Joe and Sheila's fence.

Those two gorilla-shaped pieces of poo are in so much TROUBLE because they have done graffiti saying:

Man Unitd r the bSt

"GET INSIDE!" Max bellows.

Germery comes in first. Even he looks shocked. Rhino follows behind making a noise like a donkey with hiccoughs.

Max's eyes look like they're about to shoot out of his head and fly across the ceiling.

GROOGLING FLUFFLE-EENAS!

"Why," Max yells at them, "do you think you had the right to spray paint on that fence?"

"We . . . " Germery starts. "We thought you'd like it. Because you support Manchester United."

"Listen," Mum says, and her voice is sooo cross, "you do *not* go around spraying paint on other peoples' fences."

Germery shrugs his shoulders and shouts back, "And you don't go around telling us what to do. Mum says we don't have to listen to you."

"Well, I am telling you now, Jeremy Warburton," Mum says in a whisper that carries a million atoms of anger with it, "you are going to apologise to Joe and Sheila because that fence is theirs and not ours. You are going round now. With your father."

Germery looks at her like she is a bucket of vomit. For one second nobody moves. Nobody says anything.

Then Max grabs Germery's shoulders, and his voice is not as quiet as Mum's. "You, Jeremy, are going to say sorry to Sharon. Then you are coming with me to say sorry to Joe and Sheila."

"I hate you," Germery shouts at Mum. "You only married Dad because you couldn't find anyone else and wanted his money."

Mum's mouth opens. Her mouth closes. It opens again, a bit like a goldfish. She looks at

131

Max and says very quietly, "I'm going upstairs. You can deal with your sons how you see fit."

When they return from saying sorry to Joe and Sheila, Max lets the baboons go on the PlayStation because he wants to tip-toe upstairs and see Mum.

He is such a PUSHOVER!

He closes the bedroom door so I can't hear what they say.

"I want a biscuit," Rhino says.

"You can't have one," I say.

"I want one as well," Germery says.

"I'm in charge of you and neither of you are having one."

Germery stands up and fetches the biscuit tin from the kitchen. He takes the lid off. I try to snatch it out of his hands but he grabs it back and biscuits shoot all over the place.

"That's your fault," Germery says, and his eyes lock on to mine while he moves his left foot over one of the biscuits lying on the carpet. Then he twists his heel until the biscuit is nothing but crumbs.

Those biscuits are my favourites. Mum

bought two packets: one went in the tin, the other she gave to me to keep in my bedroom so the boys couldn't get them.

There'll be more shouting and yelling when Mum and Max see what Germery's done. I don't want that. I don't want Mum upset any more. I have to do something to stop it. I am SOOO sick of them and how they SPOIL EVERYTHING.

"If you help me put the biscuits back in the tin," I say, "and eat it off a plate, I won't tell you've had one."

The two baboon-faced monsters look at each other, then at me.

"Get the brush and pan then," I say to Germery. "It's under the sink." He stares at me like he is making up his mind whether to go. Then he turns and walks towards the kitchen door.

When Max returns downstairs, the carpet has no crumbs and the biscuit tin is back on the shelf. All three of us have eaten a biscuit and put our plates back in the kitchen. I have also made some tea in the teapot and got two mugs ready. There is lots of milk in one and a little bit of milk in the other. I take them upstairs on Mum's favourite tray. It has red roses on it. Max gave it to her for her birthday.

Mum is sitting on her bed, leaning against two pillows. She has been crying.

"I hoped you'd come," she whispers as I cuddle up to her. "I can't make Ryan and Jeremy love me and I don't want to take Kelly's place, but I can't take much more of this."

"Mum," I whisper as she strokes my hair, "why doesn't Max make them behave themselves?"

"When he was growing up, his mum did the telling off and his dad did the treats. So that's what he thinks dads should do. Kelly walked out when they were little and left him to look after them. Those boys lived on treats."

"I hate it when they come back from Kelly's," I say.

"So do I," she whispers. "But she's their mum and they need to spend time with her, even though she fills their heads with horrible things about me."

I feel tears bubbling in my eyes and Mum whispers, "I know," in my ear, and I wonder what she knows when I don't even know myself.

"I . . . I . . . I thought Max would become my dad," I whisper. And the next words just pop out of my mouth: "But I've got a mum and a Max."

"I know," she whispers. "I know."

CHAPTER 18

As I wake up I imagine what I sooo want to happen:

```
FADE IN:

EXTERNAL LOCATION - PEDDLE-WORTH
VILLAGE GREEN - MORNING

JULIA and CHARLIE drink Swimmy
Bear milkshakes outside the
village shop. A brand new BMW
glides towards them. It stops and
a tall, dark-haired man wearing
shades, AL SMITH, gets out.
```

Charlie knows who it is and
stands up.

AL SMITH

[Smiling, holding his arms out]

Charlie! Are you really my
daughter?

CHARLIE

[Laughing, happy, excited,
running into his arms]

Dad!

FADE OUT

I chat to Mum while I make chocolate brownies.
We're having them for pudding this evening.
She leaves her ironing to help me measure the
sugar correctly. As she does, Rhino races through
the kitchen door and slams into the ironing
board. It topples over. Rhino clatters on top of it,
then lets out the biggest scream I have ever
heard. Germery, who was chasing him, stands in

the doorway as Mum throws herself across the kitchen to pull the iron off Rhino's tummy.

"Charlie," she says, "run the cold water tap and put a clean tea towel under it. Jeremy, turn the iron off at the switch. Ryan, I'm going to put cold water on your burn to cool it."

I move to the sink. Germery moves to the plug. Rhino gasps for breath. Mum puts the iron down on the floor, facing the wall, then sits next to Rhino.

"Charlie, squeeze out the tea towel then bring it over here."

Rhino screams as Mum lays it on his burn.

"Ryan," Mum says, "the burn will stop hurting sooner if doctors and nurses look after it. Charlie, phone Max and tell him to meet us at A and E."

Max is waiting by the hospital car park entrance. "I want my mummy," Rhino screams as he opens the car door.

"If it's bad," Max says, helping Rhino out of his car seat, "we'll contact her. OK?"

"I'll phone Mum now," Germery says, and pulls out the blue mobile from his pocket.

"Kelly'll love that," Mum says, and Max goes, "If Ry wants his—"

"Shall I leave now, or later?" Mum says, cutting right across him. It's like she's spitting in Max's face.

Max mutters something, scoops Rhino out of the car and walks across the car park with him. Germery kicks a stone as he wanders behind them.

I want to go home. I never want to see Rhino or Germery again. Or Max. But Mum is saying, "We need a car park ticket. The machine's over there. If I give you the money, can you go and get it?"

"Do we have to stay?" I whisper.

"We do. Those two boys need a proper mum and I am the best they are going to get. We stay." She takes a deep breath. "Charlie, are you all right with that?"

My mum writes fairy notes and buys me biscuits and makes chocolate brownies with me and helps me with my homework and smiles when I tell her about the Milkshake Detectives. She plays Cluedo with me when the boys watch football and chats to me when we are in the shop. I love her so much. And I hate it when the baboons are rude to her. Right now she needs me to buy a parking ticket. So I take the money she is holding out and walk across the car park.

The chairs in A&E are blue and very uncomfortable. A woman opposite us has a tea towel around her hand. Someone else looks like they are about to be sick. People keep walking in and out of the big swing doors. Nurses call names out but Ryan Warburton's name is never one of them.

Germery points at the vending machine by the big swing doors and says, "I want chocolate."

"Not now," Max says.

"I've got some chocolate biscuits in my bag," Mum says. "Would you like one?"

"No," Germery says. "I want something from the machine. Not you."

Max looks at him then looks at Mum. Max looks at Germery again and takes a coin out of his pocket.

When Germery returns from the vending machine, he undoes the wrapper, drops it on the floor then stands next to Rhino and Max while he eats it.

"Well! Look who's arrived!" Mum says and her eyes are glaring at the swing doors. "Your mum's here, Ryan."

Kelly is wearing a dark green jumper that is nearly the same colour as the one Mum is wearing. She walks with a slight limp and her hair is swept up on top of her head. She smiles at Germery and holds her arms out as he runs to her.

"She threw the iron at Ry," Germery says, in a very loud voice.

"Sharon did not," Max says, just as loudly, but now everyone's heads are turning towards us. They watch as Kelly sits on the seat next to Rhino and gives Mum one of the filthiest looks I have ever seen. Rhino tries to climb off Max's lap and on to Kelly's.

"No, darling," Kelly whispers. "You'll crease my skirt and I have to go on to a reception in an art gallery."

Mum's eyes widen.

"How bad is the burn?" Kelly asks Max.

"I got a wet tea towel on it as soon as Ryan ran into the ironing board," Mum says very

141

calmly. "Then I protected it with cling film. The burn is not as bad as it could have been."

"But why were you ironing when the boys were around?" Kelly says.

"Jeremy chased Ryan into the kitchen," Mum answers. "I told them I was ironing, like I always do."

"So are you blaming Jeremy because you weren't looking after my children properly?"

"No," Mum says. "I'm just making sure you understand what happened when one of your children hurt himself. It's what a good mother would want to know."

"And what do you mean by that?" Kelly snaps.

"What I mean," Mum says, "is that children need parents who understand what is happening to them."

"And do you understand my children?" Kelly says.

"I think I probably do," Mum says and stands up. Her handbag is over her shoulder as if she is leaving.

Max stares at her, like he doesn't want her to go. But he still says nothing.

Mum looks at Rhino. "Now your mum's here," she says, "I'm going to let her and your dad take care of you. Keep being brave and I'll see you when you come back to Peddle-Worth."

She turns to Germery and says, "I'll see you when you come back home." Then she turns to me and says, "Shall we go?", and I stand up because where Mum goes, I go too.

CHAPTER 19

We walk back to the car. Mum unlocks the doors and we get in. Tears roll down her cheeks. "I can't do this any longer," she whispers, and the words come out in a choking gasp.

I've seen her sad-upset, like when Gramma died.

I've seen her angry-upset, like when I drew all over the sofa in the flat with felt-tip pen.

I've seen her hurt-upset, like when she fell over and twisted her ankle.

I've seen her upset-upset, like when she went for a job and didn't get it.

But I've never seen her like this.

This is like she's about-to-give-up-upset and I

don't know what to do, so I start crying as well, because at that moment I am her BEST FRIEND. If we were at home I'd write her a fairy note. It would say:

Dear Mum,
  I can't do this any longer either.
Love,
Charlie xxxxxxxxx

The fairy box isn't here, though, so I just say the words out loud. "Mum, I can't do this any longer either."

"Max and I thought we could bring our two families together," she says quietly. "But it's not happening, is it?"

"I hate them," I say.

"I know," Mum says. "But thank you for trying to like them."

That makes me feel a bit guilty because, actually, I've never really tried to like Rhino and Jeremy. Ever. I hated them from the first time I saw them.

"Why do they have to fight me all the time?" Mum says, almost to herself, as a silver car drives past looking for somewhere to park. "Why does Kelly have to do everything she possibly can to turn them against me?"

We sit for a few more minutes. The silver car drives past us again. It's still looking for somewhere to park. Mum turns on the car engine.

"Let's go and see Billy and Maria," she murmurs. "They'll know what to do."

When Mum sees Maria, she starts crying all over again.

"You go in the kitchen," Maria says to Mum. "Charlie, come upstairs with me."

At the top of the stairs is a room with two huge sofas, a whopping-sized screen and a projector hanging from the ceiling.

"It's like a cinema!" I say.

"I know," Maria says. "Billy and I love watching films. Choose one and I'll put it on for you." She points at a bookcase stacked with DVDs. "Children's films are over there."

Madagascar is on the second shelf down. Maria switches the projector on then hands me the remote. "Stay up here," she says. "Sounds like you've had a long day." She hurries back downstairs.

I look around the room. My eyes stop when they come to the five DVDs of *The Jungle Book* lying on the table. I think, The Jungle Book *has a character in it that is a bear. Baloo the bear. Billy and Maria. The prize for the Bear Hunt . . .*

This is interesting!

Maria is now in the kitchen. I turn the volume down so I can hear what's happening downstairs.

"Everything in me wants to leave," Mum sobs. "No matter what I do, those boys still hate me. And what's all this doing to Charlie?"

"You've played a game of Happy Families with real children," Maria says, "and everyone has different rules. Especially Kelly."

"Don't I know it," Mum says. "But what do I do?"

I never find out what Maria thinks Mum should do because the front door opens, and a few seconds later Billy's voice asks Mum what's happened. When she tells him, he says something really RUDE about Rhino and Germery (which I agree with). My ears strain to hear more but they are talking too quietly. Then there are footsteps on the stairs, so I turn the volume back up, look at the screen and also start texting Julia to tell her what has happened and arrange to meet up tomorrow.

Billy and I only watch a bit of *Madagascar* because Mum appears and says we are going home.

Back at Dead End Lane, she and I drink cups of tea and eat biscuits while she sends texts to Max and he sends texts back. The boys and he finally get home at twelve minutes past eleven. Rhino has special cream to put on his burn and he must be careful with it for a few weeks. We all go to bed then; but Mum and Max talk in low voices for ages, and Germery thumps his wrist against my wall so I can't go to sleep.

I clutch Bertie and hope my real dad writes to me tomorrow. I want him to say I can go and live with him.

CHAPTER 20

"You all right?" Mum says, as I pour cereal into
my bowl the next day.

I nod, though I am feeling the most FED UP I
have ever felt in MY WHOLE LIFE.

"Yesterday was a turning point," Mum says.
"We are going to make this work."

All I say is, "I'm meeting Julia in ten
minutes."

"OK," Mum says. "Be back in time for lunch.
I'm doing pizzas."

I shovel my cereal down, brush my teeth as
quickly as I can then get out of the house. Julia
is waiting at the bottom of Keepers Close.

As we walk towards the allotments I tell her

about yesterday, especially about seeing the five *Jungle Book* DVDs in Billy and Maria's house.

"I think that's the prize," Agent J says.

"It might be," I say, "but it's not unique, though."

"Perhaps they're going to put something with them?" she says. "Like the DVDs are just part of the prize." Then she asks how Rhino is.

"Watching telly when I left," I answer. "Mum's got to take him to the doctor's today to get him checked."

There's nothing new at the allotments, but as we walk back down the road, two boys on bikes ride out of Oli's house. Julia's face goes bright red like a chilli pepper and she twitches her head to make sure her hair is dangling down, off her shoulders. *Bats don't come out at night, either.*

"Hiya," Oli calls out, screeching his bike brakes as he stops. Stevie does the same and they perch on their saddles, waiting for us to reach them.

"Have you just been up to the allotments?" Stevie asks.

"Yes," I say, because Julia is tongue-tied. Honestly, I can't take her anywhere! "There's nothing up there."

"But there was!" Stevie says.

"When?"

"Last night. We were doing wheelies in Oli's front garden and the Bear ran up the road. So we rode after him."

"Him?" I say. "Are you sure it's a man?"

"Definitely."

"What time?"

"Half past seven. Just before it got dark."

"Did you catch him?"

"No. He had a key for the allotment. He let himself in, locked the gate again, then stood a metre away from us, waving."

"What? You were that close?"

"Yup. Then he walked down the path behind the hedge. We watched for a while for when he came out, but we had to be back home by eight o'clock so we had to leave him in there."

"Did he leave the next clue?"

"Nope," Stevie says. "Oli's mum thinks we scared him off."

"So who do you think the Bear is?" I ask.

"We're not sure," Stevie says.

"Tell us your suspects," Agent J says, "and we'll tell you ours."

151

I shoot my eyes to take in her face. It's still bright red but at least she can talk. "Like, we'll swap info," I add. "It'll help all of us win the prize."

"And what do you think the prize is?" Oli says.

"Trip to the zoo to feed a bear," I say. "What do you think?"

"A voucher or honey or a book about bears," Stevie says. "It won't be anything massive. This whole Bear thing is just a bit of fun. The adults are enjoying it as much as we are."

"Go on, then," Agent J pleads. "Tell us who you think the Bear is."

"Mr Kahn," Oli says.

"Mr Kahn?" she repeats.

"He was on the field earlier than usual when Arthur found the football under the hedge. So we think Mr Kahn put it there. He also has a gnome with a fishing rod in his garden, exactly the same as the one in the oak tree with the first clue."

FLOOFFLING FLUDGLING!

"Your turn now," Stevie says. "Who do you think it is?"

"Maria," Agent J says straight away. I look at her. She knows it can't possibly be Maria because she was in her house yesterday evening when Mum and I went round.

"Maria knows everyone and they're selling bear biscuits and bear milkshakes and making money out of it."

Stevie and Oli look at each other. Agent J looks at them too. (She doesn't get both of them this close very often and is making the most of it.)

"Who else do you think the Bear is?" Agent J asks

"Your dad," Stevie says to Julia. Now that is a new one!

"My dad!" Julia says.

"Yup. So he can write articles about it in the newspaper. When the football clue was found, your dad was there taking photos of us all."

DOUBLE FLOOFFLING FLUDGLING! They're right. He was!

"We've given you two names," Oli asks. "You need to give us one more."

"Your mum," I say to Stevie.

"My mum!" Stevie says. "Why?"

"We saw her with a lollipop the same day the Tumble Tots got them."

"She's always eating lollipops," Stevie says, and I think, *But I can't remember seeing any in her office.*

Julia would have stayed there all day, but Oli and Stevie have to be somewhere and ride off.

"Bye," Julia calls out after them, then turns to me with a dreamy smile on her face. Thankfully the next words out of her mouth are quite sensible. "So which of our suspects has an allotment key?" she says.

"I've never heard Billy or Maria talk about doing things on the allotment," I say. "But Stevie's mum's walked over the bridge wearing wellies."

"Wouldn't Stevie have said something about it?" Agent J says.

"I don't know," I say. "We didn't tell them that our number one prime suspect is William Holdsworth's mum. Maybe they didn't tell us everything either." Suddenly my brain is splitting open with a new thought and I'm cross I didn't think of it before. "What was William Holdsworth's mum wearing that day we looked after Fluffles outside the shop?"

Agent J's mouth drops. "Wellies," she says.

"And do you remember her hands when she tied the lead around your chair?"

Agent J's eyes light up. "They were muddy!" she says. "I bet William Holdsworth's mum has an allotment key!"

"But I don't think William Holdsworth's mum would be able to run fast, which is what Freya and Millie said he did," I say. "She walks everywhere very slowly."

"You're right, she does," Agent J says.

We walk back to the allotments, lean our notebooks on the top of the gate and write out yet ANOTHER new list of suspects. William Holdsworth's mum is in top place.

"Billy was out when Oli and Stevie spotted the Bear," I say.

"I bet he had his bear costume on!" Agent J says.

"He came straight up the stai— no, he didn't," I say. "He was in the kitchen for several minutes before he came upstairs."

"Enough time to take off a bear costume?" Agent J asks.

I nod my head.

"Billy's a definite suspect then," she says. "But does he have an allotment key?"

"Not that I know of," I say. "But" – something else is tumbling over in my mind – "you know when we saw William Holdsworth's mum and Maria after the sleepover at your house ... Maria said the cat woke HER up. She never mentioned Billy. He could have been out, being the Bear."

"Maria and Billy don't have any children," Agent J says. "And this whole Bear Hunt is for children."

"But Billy likes children and knows what children in the village do, and he sells things for children in the shop," I say. Then I add, "Or it could be Mr Kahn. He has a little boy and we now know he owns a fishing rod gnome. He can run fast as well."

"Definite suspect then, after William Holdsworth's mum, and Billy," Agent J says. "But does he have an allotment key?"

We don't know the answer to that question.

"Rev Proctor?" I say. "Is she a suspect?"

"She helps," Agent J says. "But I don't think she is the Bear."

"What about your dad?" I say.

"No," Agent J says. "Definitely, definitely not him."

"But we ought to write his name down," I say. So we write his name next to my mum's name.

"Wouldn't we be useless detectives if it was either of our parents!" Agent J says, and we look at each other and giggle.

After supper, Max and Mum tell me, Rhino and Germery to go into the living room and sit on the sofa.

"Why?" Germery says.

"Just do it," Max says. Rhino moves very carefully and sits with a cushion on his lap as he says that helps his tummy (I'm not sure why). Mum and Max sit in the armchairs opposite us. This is serious.

"We have thought hard about what happened in A and E," Max says.

"We've written down what we want to say," Mum says. "We know it has been difficult getting used to each other, but there are going to be changes in how we behave."

Max then reads from a piece of paper he takes out of his pocket.

FOR THE BOYS:

1. If Kelly says anything about Sharon, you will not repeat it.

2. In Peddle-Worth, you will do what Sharon says.

3. There will be no more farting at or back-chatting Sharon.

4. You will be polite, and food will be eaten with knives, forks and spoons.

5. No shouting and screaming, unless you are watching football.

I like the sound of all that. But now Mum takes out a piece of paper as well and turns to me.

"Charlie," she says, and I frown because it's not my fault those freaks are so badly behaved. "From now on you are only going to Julia's twice a week. You are not running away from this family. We are going to make this work and do things together until we like each other. You are going to stop calling the boys Rhino and Germery."

As she says that, Germery sticks his tongue out at me and smirks.

"He can stop pulling stupid faces at me as well," I say.

"And you, Charlie, can stop trying to get him in trouble," Mum says, and I stare back at her and wish, WISH the postman would drop an envelope addressed to me through the letter box with GOOD NEWS in it.

"And he can stop banging on the bedroom wall as well," I say. "He only does that to annoy me."

"The three of you are going to stop annoying each other, full stop," Max says. "Understand?"

"Yes, Dad," Rhino says.

"Suppose so," Germery says.

"And you?" Max says to me.

"I've got it," I say, because I want everyone to leave me alone.

I wake up. It is still dark. Rhino/Ryan is shouting in his sleep. He does that from time to time.

Tonight he is calling out, "Mummy!" and crying.

Someone walks across the landing and into the front bedroom. Max's voice murmurs but Ryan carries on crying and now Jeremy is awake and crying as well. More footsteps cross the landing. Then I hear Mum's voice singing very quietly.

FLOOPLE-POPS! She's singing them the song she used to sing to me when I couldn't get to sleep. She used to stroke my head as she sang it. I bet she's stroking Ryan's head.

But it's MY song. Not theirs.

I lie in bed listening to it. I bet Max is sitting on Jeremy's bed. It's so NOT FAIR.

I guess that song's not just mine any more. It's theirs as well.

Come on postman. Bring me a letter from my dad.

CHAPTER 21

Next day, there's STILL nothing at the allotments.

"I think William Holdsworth's mum will be out tonight," Agent J says. "She went at half past eight in the evening last time. We have to watch her. Can we have a sleepover at your house and watch from the front bedroom?"

"If we do, I'll have to tell the baboons," I say. "I don't want to do that!"

"Why not?"

"They're horrible."

"They're not that bad," Agent J says.

"They are!" I say.

"This is Milkshake Detectives business," she says. "And if we see William Holdsworth's mum dressed up in a bear costume coming out of her front door, we'll know it definitely is her and we can follow her and get to the clues first and win the prize."

So in the end I agree.

My Penelope Pink and Sabrina Scarlett stickers guard Julia's bag while we are downstairs. At half past seven, when the boys go to bed, we go up as well and put on our PJs and dressing gowns. Once Mum and Max are downstairs with the telly on, we sneak across the landing.

"Shhhh!" I whisper as Agent J and I go into their bedroom.

"What do you want?" Jeremy says.

"We need your help," Agent J whispers. "Can you keep an absolute secret?"

"Perhaps."

"It's about the Bear. We think she lives in Dead End Lane," I whisper.

"She's probably going to the allotments tonight," Agent J says. "We want to look out of your window."

"We'll be eating biscuits," I say, and show them a packet of my favourite ones. That works.

"But you MUST NOT say anything about this to ANYONE," Agent J says.

"We won't," Jeremy says, looking at the biscuits again.

"Promise?" Julia says.

"Promise," the boys both say together.

Outside, it is starting to get dark.

"We ought to have a plate for these biscuits," I say, opening the wrapper. The card Kelly sent the boys when we first moved here is lying at one end of the window sill. Agent J picks it up.

"This'll do," she says. I count out eight biscuits and put them on the card. As I do, Ryan says, "I can't see out of the window."

"You need something to stand on then, don't you," Agent J replies, and looks around the room. Jeremy has a table next to his bed with his torch and latest Lego truck on. "Can I shove your things on the floor?" she asks him.

"All right," Jeremy says and, a minute later, Agent J carefully lifts Ryan on to the table next to her. I stand on the other side of her and then there is Jeremy. We are ready to see the Bear!

"Can you get the phone?" Ryan whispers to Agent J. He points at the blue mobile lying on his pillow.

"Lazy legs," she says to him. "Who's going to phone you?"

"My mummy," he whispers.

"Ry, she won't phone," Jeremy says.

"She promised she would," Ryan whispers.

"She promised she'd come to see me in my assembly at school and never came. Sharon came instead."

"Maybe she'll phone tomorrow," Agent J says.

"Nah. She won't," Jeremy says. "But she will buy us something next Saturday to make up for it. I want a radio-controlled car like William's got."

"I want my mummy," Ryan says, and his voice is trembling like he is going to cry and I'm sooo glad my mum isn't like their mum. I bet Kelly doesn't have fairy boxes or plays Cluedo or makes cupcakes.

"Would another biscuit help?" I whisper, shoving Kelly's card towards him. Ryan's clutching the blue mobile like Kelly will feel him holding it and remember to phone him.

"I've got some marshmallows as well," Agent J says. "And some lemonade." She and I were going to save those for later on when it was just me and her, but I'm pleased she thought of getting them now.

"Only give Ry a little bit so he doesn't wet himself," Jeremy whispers to Julia as she pours the lemonade. She stops pouring completely though, because Ryan is suddenly stabbing the air in front of him, his eyes wide.

We look at where he is pointing.

DOOFA-WOOBLINGTON!

Walking down William Holdsworth's drive is a figure dressed in a bear costume!

THE BEAR *MUST* BE WILLIAM HOLDSWORTH'S MUM!

But then *another* bear walks down her drive.

DOUBLE DOOFA-WOOBLINGTON!!

THERE ARE *TWO* OF THEM!!

"Let's go and get them!" Jeremy says, stuffing his second biscuit in his dressing-gown pocket and heading for the bedroom door.

Agent J and I look at each other in the half-light. She nods her head. So do I. It is time to meet the Bears, and this is going to be sooo brilliant.

A little "Uh-ugh" noise comes from Jeremy's table. Ryan is holding his arms out to be lifted down. My arms slot under his armpits to pick him up. Then I pull them back.

"Shall we leave your mobile up here in case you drop it?" I say.

"But my mummy might phone and I'll miss her," he whispers.

"Ry, she's not going to phone." His eyes are level with mine as I gently take his fingers off the phone and put it next to the biscuit crumbs on top of Kelly's card. Then I carefully lift him down. Somehow his hand slips into mine and we tip-toe down the stairs together behind Jeremy and Agent J.

We're not quiet enough, though. Mum comes out of the living room and asks us where we think we are going.

"To see the bears," Jeremy says. "They're outside."

"There are two of them," Agent J says.

"Two?" Mum says, and we all nod and I am thinking, *Hurry up! We're going to miss them!*

Mum calls out to Max, "It'll be all right if they go and say hello to the Bear, won't it?" And before Max answers, she carries on, "But no further than our house, OK?"

"OK," we say.

Jeremy and Agent J charge down the drive and jump out in front of the two bears. Ryan and I are just behind them.

One of the bears says, "Oooh! Hello!" IN WILLIAM HOLDSWORTH'S MUM'S VOICE.

But the other bear says nothing.

"Where are you going?" Jeremy asks them, but neither bear says a word.

"Are you going to the allotments?" Agent J asks.

The bears shrug their shoulders.

"Why are there two of you?" I ask but all they do is shrug again.

Then Ryan takes a step forward to touch the bear that's not William Holdsworth's mum. He (or she) takes a step backwards, and William Holdsworth's mum says, "No touching."

Then the two bears walk around us, wave and carry on down Dead End Lane.

"The one we don't know is a man," Agent J says.

"Definitely," I agree with her.

"It's a man," Jeremy says.

"It's a bear man," Ryan says, and we all laugh.

"Do you think William knows his mum's a bear?" Agent J asks as she and I lie, wide awake, in my bedroom.

"Dunno," I say. "But I think the other bear is either Billy or Mr Kahn."

"Do you think Oli will see them walking past his house?"

"Oli," I whisper. "Are you there, looking out of your window?"

"I don't fancy him," she says. *Bananas aren't yellow, either.*

"Tomorrow morning, we go to the allotments as soon as we wake up," I say.

"And then I must go home," Agent J says. She must be home by half past nine because she and her dad and mum and Emily are going to a film premiere in London and meeting some of the actors.

I wish something exciting like that would happen to me.

*

Next morning, Agent J and I run to the allotments. A barrel, full of apples, is by the allotment gate with a note on blue paper hanging from the handles.

Share these with someone you like.

To find the Bear's lair,

You must go up a stair.

"What do you think it means?"

"We need to think of places with stairs. The bridge has a ramp, so it can't be the bridge."

"The church has steps up the tower," Agent J says. "That would make the second bear Rev Proctor."

"She's not a man," I say, "though she is Stevie's mum and the clue says to share the apples with someone you like. You could take one to Stevie and one to Oli."

Julia completely ignores me and says, "Who would you give an apple to, then?"

For some reason I think of last night and little Ryan standing on Jeremy's table in his dressing-gown, clutching his mobile phone.

Kelly's their real mum but my mum's their proper mum. At Kelly's they watch telly and play on their PlayStation. She buys them things but she doesn't do their washing and doesn't want them when they're ill. She didn't even give Ryan a cuddle when he was in A&E. She should have done, shouldn't she? That's what mums do. It wasn't fair on him.

"I'm taking apples for Ryan and Jeremy," I say.

"What? Do you actually like them now?" Julia says.

"No," I say. *The sky isn't blue either, is it?* And the thought surprises me. My next thought does, too: "When we saw William Holdsworth's mum and the other bear, they weren't carrying anything last night. So how did this barrel of apples get here?"

"Agent C," Agent J squeals back, "you are absolutely right. There must be a *third* bear out there somewhere!"

CHAPTER 22

There's a note in the fairy box.

Dear Charlie,
    Thank you for bringing the apples for Ryan and Jeremy.
    Love,
    Mum xxxxxxx

I leave a reply:

Dear Mummy,
    Do you know how many bears there are and who they are?
    Love,
    Charlie xxxxxx

After lunch, Max takes the boys to town to buy new trainers. Mum and Maria are going to the warehouse. I don't want to go, so I stay with Billy. I might live two doors down from William Holdsworth's mum, but I cannot see in her house. However, I *can* watch Billy and have another idea for a milkshake. With a bit of luck he'll make one and let me try it out.

He does. The Malty Geezer milkshake, with Maltesers in it, is the BEST yet. Rob the builder says he wants to try one when he gets back from buying some paint.

"What colour are you buying?" I ask him as he leaves the shop.

"A small pot of purple and a large one of light green," he says.

"Can I go up and have a look?" I ask Billy, when Rob has gone.

"No," he says, shaking his head. "Not until opening day."

"When's that?" I ask.

"Fairly soon." He smiles. As he does, there's a honking noise outside. "They don't give up, do they?" Billy sighs. "Do you want to Chinese takeaway them with the water pistol, or shall I?"

"I'll do it," I say.

But those brutal beasts know what a SuperSoaka is by now and quack their way back across the road as soon as I throw the shop door open. I chase them to the pond with Billy standing in the doorway laughing and cheering me on.

As I turn to walk back, there's a shivering, thumping *crack!* and the ground shudders. Above me, the huge oak tree suddenly splits, as if an invisible giant has swung his axe and chopped it in two. One half of the tree stands tall; the other half falls, very slowly, towards the shop, like it's in slow motion. All I can do is watch it topple.

The top branches hit the front of the shop and the trunk bounces as it lands, settling as an eerie silence closes in. Tables, chairs, the awning, where I walked a few seconds ago, where Billy was standing, all disappear under the tree.

No one is in the street, no one is on the bridge; the Soptons are in London, Mum and Maria are at the warehouse and Billy could be INJURED. He could be BURIED ALIVE.

I run as close as I can to the shop.

"Billy!" I call out.

But he doesn't reply.

"Billy!" I call again. Panic rises in the back of my throat. I think about what Penelope Pink would say:

PENELOPE PINK : You can do this, Agent C.

AGENT C : But I don't know what to do.

PENELOPE PINK : Yes, you do. Go around the back of the shop. Use ET's phone number. Try it on the back gate.

I run as fast as I can down the side of the shop. There's a gate in the fence with a keypad. I punch in ET5271. There's a little click. The gate opens. I've never been in the yard before. The door to the back of the shop has another keypad. ET5271. There's another click and I walk into the room where the vacuum cleaner and brushes and other cleaning things are kept.

And there, folded on the floor next to the vacuum cleaner, is a bear costume! Billy. Or Maria. One of them is DEFINITELY a Bear.

To find the Bear's lair,

You must go up a stair

The 'stair' in the clue is in the shop. The lair must be in the café! We know who to watch, who to follow! But, right now, I have to get to Billy.

In the shop there's a funny smell and glass and tins and newspapers are scattered on the floor. It's dark as well.

"Billy?" I call out, and this time he answers.

"I'm here." His voice isn't strong and loud like it usually is. "I've hurt my head and it's bleeding. Can you get me the towel from the loo? Then can you phone your mum and tell her? And be careful of all this glass."

I bring the towel to him. My bag has fallen behind the counter. I find my phone and dial Mum.

"Was anyone else in the shop?" Mum asks.

"No," I say, and my voice trembles a little bit.

"Thank goodness for that," she says. "Maria and I will be with you in twenty minutes. Can you put me on to Billy?"

I pass the phone over. He is now holding the towel over the side of his head.

"It could be worse," he says. "Charlie and I'll sit in the back yard until you get here. It's just the front pane of glass that's gone, and the outside café, of course. But I think the shop itself is OK."

When Mum and Maria arrive, Billy is still holding the towel to his head. It's covered in blood. Maria says she is taking him straight to hospital. Mum says she'll start phoning people to get the tree sorted and the front of the shop repaired.

CHAPTER 23

FADE IN:

INTERNAL LOCATION - CHARLIE'S
BEDROOM - EVENING

MUM sits on the end of CHARLIE's
bed. Behind her, the new curtains
are drawn.

MUM

[Looking straight into Charlie's
face]

I was really proud of you this
afternoon.

CHARLIE

[Looking straight back]

I could have been sitting
outside. It'd have got me then.

MUM

[Sighing]

Try not to think about it.
[Pause.] But did you notice
anything when you went in the
shop through the back door?

CHARLIE

[Pretending to frown]

Like what?

FADE OUT

"The Bear Hunt isn't quite over yet," Mum
says.

"So you do know who the bears are then?" I
ask her.

"Maybe." She smiles in a way that tells me

she does. "Who do you think they are?" she says.

"We know for sure that one is William Holdsworth's mum. The other one is either Billy or Maria. But there must be someone else who delivered the apples to the allotments because the two bears we saw in Dead End Lane weren't carrying anything."

"The Milkshake Detectives have done really well." Mum smiles and her eyes twinkle and she is chuckling. I have a feeling there is still something we haven't found out (something more than just who the third bear is).

Julia phones me at nine o'clock to tell me about London. It's a very long phone call, partly because she has fallen in love with an actor.

At school, everyone is talking about the oak tree falling down, the shop front being smashed, the Bear's clue about stairs (no one can work it out), who they gave their apples to and what they've done in the Easter holidays. No one else knows what the Milkshake Detectives know about there being more than one bear. Not even Oli and Stevie. And William

Holdsworth hasn't got a clue about anything, let alone the fact (yes, fact!) that HIS MUM and one other bear were in his house. And NO ONE AT ALL knows that the Milkshake Detectives have one agent working in the shop where the next clue is going to appear, and another doing surveillance duties!

Max collects Ryan and Jeremy and me from school because he's worked at home today.

When we get home, he says "Something arrived for you today."

My heart skips a beat as he hands me an envelope. It's white and addressed to Miss Lottie Warburton.

My dad has written to me!

Max watches as I tear the envelope open. The piece of paper I pull out is folded in two places. I uncrease the folds and lay it on the table.

Dear Lottie,
I opened the envelope as it is nine
years since Alan Smith lived here.
When we bought the house, he was about
to travel the world and left no

forwarding address. Sorry I can't be
more helpful.
Yours sincerely,
P Walters

I read the letter once. Then I read it again.
The second time is harder because the words are
all blurry.

"Not what you were hoping for?" Max
whispers, and I shake my head. "Can I have a
look?" he asks. He gently takes the letter from
my fingers and reads it. "Charlie, I'm so sorry,"
he says, and now I am crying properly. Max puts
his arm around me and holds me really tight.
"I'm sorry," he whispers. "It was really important
to you, wasn't it?"

"I ... I ... " But I can't get any more words
out.

And then Ryan's little voice says, "What's up
with Charlie?"

"She's had some bad news," Max says quietly.
"She thought she might be able to find her real
dad, but now she knows she can't."

"My dad's not there," I stutter. "He's gone."

"Oh," Ryan says again. He walks across the

kitchen to the food cupboard, takes out the biscuit tin and walks back into the living room.

"He didn't ask for a biscuit, did he?" Max mutters, almost to himself. But I don't want to think about Ryan, or Jeremy, because they have a dad AND I DON'T. I dreamed my dad was going to come back. For me. But he's not. He's travelling the world without a forwarding address. He doesn't ever want me to find him.

Ryan and Jeremy are back in the kitchen. Why can't they leave us alone? Just for one second?

They put the biscuit tin on the table.

"There's only one of your favourite biscuits left," Jeremy says. "We want you to have it."

Max decides we should all abandon doing homework and go to the shop where Mum is. The tree has been cleared, the front window repaired and this afternoon the shop reopened.

"Can we have a bear biscuit as well?" Jeremy asks, as we walk down Peddle ramp.

"As long as you eat your supper," Max says.

"What are we having?" I ask.

"Chicken stir fry."

When we get to the shop I show Mum the letter and she gives me a hug.

"I'm sorry," she says quietly, and gives me another hug. "Did Max and the boys look after you?" she whispers.

"Yes," I whisper back.

"Good," she says.

She makes a strawberry Mum's Sheep (for Jeremy), a banana Smart Tie (for Ryan) and a chocolate Malty Geezer (for me). Then she makes a latte coffee for Max. We go outside and sit down at the new tables. The half of the oak tree that was still standing had to be cut down to make it safe, and the pond looks weird without its tree next to it.

"What milkshake have you got, Charlie?" Ryan asks me. "Sharon made mine with vamina ice cream."

"Ry, the word's vanilla."

"Vamina," Ryan tries again, but he still can't say the word. It doesn't matter though, because we all know what he means and we sit in the sunshine and chat about what we've done at school. Jeremy's teacher chose him as 'Pupil of the Day', which means he will sit on a chair in assembly tomorrow. Suddenly there's a honking noise and the hard-core warrior ducks turn up with their little beaks chattering at us.

"Time for Chinese takeaway duty," I say.

"I want to do it!" Ryan says.

"Ry," Max says, "your burn's still sore. Sorry, but you're not doing it."

Ryan looks at him, then slides off his chair.

"I will take you home and you'll spoil this time together," Max says as Ryan heads for the shop door. Jeremy and I look at each other. Then we look at Max. He pushes his chair back and follows Ryan into the shop. A moment later he comes out again with Ryan in his arms. "And don't bother kicking me or biting me," Max says to him.

"That's well harsh!" Jeremy says.

"No, it's not," Max says. "You're going to learn that when I say something, I mean it."

Jeremy and I watch Max walk up the ramp. Donny and Ugly watch them go too, and then Billy's voice says, "You two want a job?" He has two SuperSoakas in his hands.

"Zappy zappy," Jeremy says, and he and I Chinese takeaway those ducks until they are back in their pond.

CHAPTER 24

Chinese takeawaying is what the Milkshake
Detectives plan to use to find out whose bear
costume it is in the shop. We reckon we will be
able to tell from its size who it belongs to: if it's
huge, it's Billy's; if it's medium, it's my mum's; if
it's small, it's Maria's.

We're being Goldilocks Detectives today.

Agent J waits in her house. I am in the shop,
sitting on the third step designing a house for my
felt owl to live in. I sit there as often as I can, in
case the Bear brings the next clue over. I'm also
waiting for the shop to empty so that only Mum
and I are in it. A lady (who has a bag with sharks

on it) takes her magazine and says goodbye to
Mum.

I text one word to Agent J.

NOW!

A minute later she walks across the grass
towards the shop. Behind her back she has
bread, which she drops in little pieces. Donny
and Ugly scramble out of the pond and follow
her to get the bread.

"Hello," Mum says, as Julia walks through the
shop door. "Did you have a nice time in London?"

"It was brilliant!" Julia says and pauses with
the shop door wide open. The ducks are now in
the shop. Julia screams and runs up the stairs to
get away from them.

"Ridiculous ducks." Mum sighs. "Do you
want to Chinese takeaway them?"

I look at Agent J and pull a face. She pulls one
back at me and we both shake our heads.

"I'll do it then," Mum says, and grins. "I've
never done it before."

"It's good fun," I say. "But you do have to

186

chase them right over to the pond, otherwise they sneak back."

Mum loads a SuperSoaka, waves it at the ducks to get them out of the shop, then heads off across the road.

As soon as she's safely away, Agent J and I shoot down the stairs and into the back cupboard. The bear costume is still there! Agent J quickly unfolds it and holds it up.

"That's Billy's size," I say.

"Billy's," Agent J agrees, and we both stroke the costume, just because we can. Then we refold it, rush back into the shop and back up the stairs.

A minute later, Mum returns, smiling, and says, "I enjoyed that." And we enjoyed finding out for certain who the second bear is! We now have to find out who the third one is. The one who took the apples to the allotment gate. (I think it's Mr Kahn.)

CHAPTER 25

Dear Charlie,
   Would you and Agent J like to
help the bears on their final mission?
   Love,
   Mum xxxxxxx

THEIR FINAL MISSION! We've just (nearly)
worked out who they are and they invite us to join
them! HOW AWESOME IS THAT! I leave a reply.

Dear Mummy,
   YES PLEASE!
   Love,
   Charlie xxxxxx

FALOOFA-WHOOFA!

I phone Julia STRAIGHT AWAY.

"This is the final thing the Bear will ever do," I say. "And the Milkshake Detectives are going to be part of it!"

On Friday evening, Julia comes to our house for supper. Ryan and Jeremy go to bed at their normal time but we stay up. At half past eight, Mum tells us it is time to get ready.

"Maria makes these," she says, and hands us a bear costume each. We put them on and look at each other's little tails and rounded ears. Mum has masks for us as well. "So tell me," she says, "who do the Milkshake Detectives think the bears are?"

"It's definitely William Holdsworth's mum," Agent J says.

"And Billy," I add, and smile as Mum's head nods.

"And ... anyone else?"

"Mr Kahn," I say.

"It has to be a man who can run fast," Agent J says.

"Would you like to meet the third bear?"
Mum says. She is teasing us.

"*Yes!*" we both say.

"He's in charge of tonight's mission," Mum
says. "Come in, bear."

Agent J and I turn towards the door. It opens.
A bear wearing a mask shuffles into the room.
We can't tell who it is.

The bear clears his throat.

And then I know who it is.

"Shall we go, Charlie Bear and Julia Bear?" he
says.

"Max!" Agent J squeals. "It's Max!"

I HAD A BEAR IN MY HOUSE ALL THE TIME
AND NEVER REALISED! And I am meant to be a
detective!

"Have fun." Mum laughs and the Milkshake
Detectives can't stop giggling because Max keeps
wiggling his bottom and doing bear dances.

"Can't *bear* to think what the neighbours are
thinking," he whispers as we dance out of our
back door. "At least we haven't got *bare*
bottoms." He giggles.

"Your dad is sooo funny," Julia whispers.

*

Outside, Max gives us large sticks of chalk.

"We're drawing bear paw prints on the pavement as if the Bear is walking towards Worth High Street," he says, "and we're writing '10.30am' in the middle of each paw." He shows us how big each print is to be.

When we reach Worth High Street, another bear (William Holdsworth's mum) is drawing paw prints as if the Bear has walked from school towards the bridge. Another bear is drawing them down Keepers Close.

"That bear's Maria," Max says.

"William Holdsworth's mum, Max, Maria, Billy," Julia whispers. "That's four bears! We thought there were only three."

We carry on drawing bear paw prints along Worth High Street, over the bridge and down the ramp to the shop. Another two bears are drawing paw prints on Peddle High Street that also lead to the shop.

"So who are those bears?" Agent J asks.

"Lindsay Proctor and Billy," Max says.

THAT MAKES FIVE!

"What about Mr Kahn?" I ask.

"He's one sometimes," Max says. "But he's

not dressed up tonight. He can run fast, so he's been going out in the day to add a bit of interest to the hunt."

"Who knows about it?" Agent J asks.

"Most of the adults in the village." Max chuckles. "We've had such fun." And now it all makes sense!

"Time you two were in bed," Max says, as we finish the last paw print outside the shop.

We all walk to Agent J's house. The ducks waddle across to say hello to us.

"Look!" Julia squeals. Donny and Ugly are big, fat shapes, but behind them are six smaller shapes.

"They're ducklings!" Max says. "Well done, Ugly and Donny!"

The little shapes wobble a bit and Donny and Ugly shoo them back towards the pond.

"That is sooo sweet!" Julia says.

Max and I wave at Tracy as she lets Julia into her house, then Max and I walk back home together.

"Enjoy that?" he asks.

"Loved it," I say.

Max's left hand is swinging by his side. If I

lifted my right hand, his fingers could curl around mine.

PENELOPE PINK: Why not?

AGENT C: He might go off travelling and leave no forwarding address.

PENELOPE PINK: I don't think he will. He isn't like that.

AGENT C: But does Max *want* to be my dad?

PENELOPE PINK: I think he probably does. Do you want to be his daughter?

Max's fingers are warm. He doesn't squeeze my hand, but neither does he let it go.

"Dad," I whisper, and the word sort of sticks in my throat. But once it is out I feel sooo happy. "What's happening tomorrow morning at the shop at 10.30?" I ask him softly.

"You'll find out tomorrow," he whispers back.

"Are the Milkshake Detectives going to get a prize for solving the Bear Hunt?" I ask.

"You'll have to wait and see," he says.

*

At 10.30 the next morning, Max is dressed in his bear costume. So am I. Jeremy and Ryan are wearing bear masks. People from all over the village are standing by a big sign outside the shop that says:

Bear with us today!

We can "bearly" wait,

Because today is the GRAND OPENING

Of the Bear's Lair

When you go up the stairs.

Speeches at 10.30 today.

There's a brown ribbon across the shop doorway, bear-shaped balloons hanging from the top of the shop window and a banner which reads:

The Bear's Lair Café is now open!

Julia is wearing her bear costume and looking after Emily while Tracy passes around plates of bear-shaped sandwiches. Jamie Sopton is interviewing everyone and making notes in his notebook. Stevie's mum (dressed as a bear) has a plate of bear biscuits. She grins at me as I take one.

A few minutes later, William Holdsworth's mum arrives with William and Fluffles. All three of them are dressed in bear costumes and have flags with bears on, which William hands out. Stevie and Oli have one each. They're standing with Arthur Rivers from Year 6 (who doesn't have one), and are giggling about something.

Julia is dying to find out what.

"Do you fancy Arthur Rivers as well?" I ask her.

"No," she says. *Milkshakes aren't made with milk, either.* She is sooo predictable!

When Billy and Maria (both dressed as bears) duck under the brown ribbon in the shop doorway, everyone starts clapping.

Maria has a microphone. "Hello!" she says. "Thank you all for turning out today. The dual carriageway split Peddle-Worth in two. Billy and

I wanted to help make our lovely village a community once more." She hands the microphone to Billy.

"So we had the idea," he says, "of making the upstairs of our shop into a café. We've worked with the vicar and other people in the community and the Bear's Lair is the prize at the end of the Bear Hunt. It's for everyone, especially children and young people who live in the village."

Everyone claps again. I'm thinking, *The café is unique and it's the prize ... but it's not just for us. The prize is for everyone.* I feel a bit disappointed, but I keep on smiling so no one will know.

And then Billy says, "We'd like to ask the Milkshake Detectives to step forward."

Agent J looks at me. I look at Agent J. We did not expect this; but Jamie Sopton did, because he is next to us and taking our photograph.

"Lots of children have worked on the clues the Bear has left, but these two young ladies have probably worked the hardest. They hit on the idea of trying to work out who the Bear is, which was very confusing for them as there were so many of us! We would like to ask them to cut the ribbon this morning and open the Bear's Lair Café. When they have done that, they can go upstairs and try out the prize."

Agent J and I both raise our heads in excitement. There IS a prize! *But what is it?*

"The prize," Billy says, "is to have a new milkshake named after you. Maria and I are going to call it Detective Milkshake. Anyone who wants to try one, come up the stairs to the Bear's Lair Café!"

"What's in the Detective Milkshake?" someone calls out.

"That" – Billy laughs – "is for you to work out when you drink it!"

That is sooooo MAGNIFICENTLY WICKEDLY BRILLIANT!

Maria hands us each a pair of scissors and tells us to snip the brown ribbon at the same time. As everyone claps, Billy says, "Can we have a photograph of the Milkshake Detectives with their families?"

Jamie hands his camera to Maria and stands

with Tracy and Emily next to Julia. I stand by Julia with my mum, Jeremy, Ryan and . . . MY DAD.

"Smile!" Maria says.

And we all do.

ABOUT THE AUTHOR

Heather Butler grew up in a vicarage, which meant her life was filled with a tapestry of random and interesting characters. But what influenced her most was her mum, who could create stories from thin air.

Heather is a primary teacher. When her sons were little they often brought toys and other objects to her to be included in bedtime stories. Her sons grew older, but Heather carried on creating stories. Today she teaches part-time, writes and leads writing workshops across the UK. Her first book, *Us Minus Mum*, was published by Little, Brown Young Readers in 2014. *The Milkshake Detectives* is her second book.

For details about Heather, readers' resource pack about this book, her writing, days visiting schools and a very child-friendly blog, visit: www.heatherbutler.info

ACKNOWLEDGEMENTS

Thank you to:

My husband, Derek, for your love, patience and creative support while this book was being written.

Tom, Sarah, Esme, Toby, Hannah and Reuben for being part of my immediate family; you know how important my family is to me.

Liz and Lance Hale who came with us to the Checkpoint Charlie Museum in Berlin. It was there that I saw a photograph of eight amazing octogenarians who dug a tunnel under the Berlin Wall. Their faces and what they did inspired the first ideas for the story.

Bev Reader for eating lunch with me. Ducks displaying razor-sharp teeth waddled towards us. "I bet they'll appear in a book," you said, and they did.

The children at Manor Farm Community Junior School in Hazlemere, Bucks for giving invaluable feedback about the characters and what happened to them.

My agent, Penny Holroyde, for excellent guidance and support throughout.

My editor at Little, Brown Young Readers, Kate Agar, for your help, insight, patience, guidance, Maltesers and continual chirpiness. Thank you as well to the whole team at Hachette Children's Group.